HYBRID, SCIENCE FICTION, COMEDY

illustrated

Keith Hulse

Copyright © 2023 Keith Hulse

All rights reserved

The characters and events portrayed in this book are fictitious. Any similarity to real persons, living or dead, is coincidental and not intended by the author.

No part of this book may be reproduced, or stored in a retrieval system, or transmitted in any form or by any means, electronic, mechanical, photocopying, recording, or otherwise, without express written permission of the publisher.

ISBN-9798327961500

Cover design by: Art Painter
Library of Congress Control Number: 2018675309
Printed in the United States of America

*To The Three Stooges
and funny folk everywhere.
laughter is the best medicine.*

CONTENTS

Title Page
Copyright
Dedication
Chapter 3 – SAUCER COMAND   36
Chapter 4 Dorothy   45
Chapter 5 The Great Escape   48
Chapter 6 Dorothy Arrives   69
Chapter 7 A Council   86
Chapter 8 Ex Terrestrial Highway   106
Chapter 9 Saucer Command Again   116
Chapter 10 Monsters   118
Chapter 11 The Last Supper   134
Chapter 12 The Great Escape   149
Chapter 13 Greys   160
Chapter 14 Saucer Command 4   172
Chapter 15 Loose Ends   187
Chapter 16 Fig   201
Chapter 17 End   213

Contents

Chapter 1............I am here.................... 4
Chapter 2...   ......Green Cheese............... 13
Chapter 3......   ...Saucer Command........... 29
Chapter 4...   ......Dorothy........ 36
Chapter 5............The Great Escape.................39
Update ....Saucer Command 2......... 50
Chapter 6... ....Dorothy Arrives............. ... 56
Chapter 7.............A Council...   71
Chapter 8......... .. Ex Terrestrial Highway... 87
Chapter 9......... ..Saucer Command 2...... 95
Chapter 10............Monsters...... 96
Chapter 11... ....The Last Supper...... 109
Chapter 12...... .....The Great Escape...... ... .119
Chapter 13............Greys.................. 128
Chapter 14............Saucer Command 4... 138
Chapter 15......... .Loose Ends......... ... .150
Chapter 16......... ..Fig.............. 162
Chapter 17 ....End 173

HYBRID, SCIENCE FICTION COMEDY

BY

Keith Hulse

54842 words 176 pages

HYBRID, COMEDY SCIENCE FICTION

Keith Hulse
Aberdeen
Lugbooks@gmail.com

[CHAPTER 1] – I AM HERE

Beag

As told by me, Hybrid, before I changed my name to Hybrid as such a name implies mystery.

The wonderous shiny flying saucer came to an abrupt halt in the sunset of the Pacific Ocean on a Californian beach.

A postcard scene.

Beautiful people no longer playing net ball now lounged on the sand waiting for burgers, from a campfire, no, from a lucky aspiring burger seller who had driven up with doorbell chimes singing 'Banna Split,' announcing his arrival, and on his vehicle roof a giant wobbling ice cream with a chocolate stick in it.

Every fifteen minutes little miniature tea cakes with human arms, legs and faces circled this monstrosity banging cymbals to the tune of nothing except to announce fifteen minutes had passed.

"Sweet and Sour Chicken Burger," his drone from above. He had many burgers frying, and he froze when he saw the flying saucer.

Would you freeze if you saw one close or run a mile the other way?

The vendor forgot about his one-thousand-dollar drone that flew out to the choppy sea.

The beautiful people full of smoking 'funny socks' jumped up and ran towards the alien craft. Oblivious to the fact they might be abducted, dissected, the girls made to carry alien babies, and have no memory of how they became pregnant and sent back to Earth with a wallet full of cash, see, aliens were generous folk. The boys, well if you were an alien why did you want a male human?

For dirty jobs such as plumbing blocked latrines, draining the fat from the ship's mess deep fryer, and learning sword swallowing acts to impress the alien audience at dinner.

Impress or you will be dinner as we all know aliens eat humans, steal our jobs, abduct our women, and walk amongst us as if they were angels, *what a bunch of losers right?*

I mean the sword swallowers not the aliens, have you ever swallowed a sword, oh so messy.

Anyway, "Why am I getting the bung here?" I pleaded outside the flying saucer looking towards the doorway of the flying saucer.

Figures appeared; some were holding suitcases which they threw down flooring me.

Crawling from under them I looked at bare human feet covered in sand. Looking up I followed my gaze up a leg and swallowed, it was a human girl.

"It is not green or little," a man spoke next to her meaning me.

"Either is this leg," as I followed the leg up and "slap," the dream broken by a sharp pain.

"Do aliens have girls?" The author of the slap, a skinny man dressed as a tramp under a learning on a cane.

'BEACH BUM,' was written on a cardboard piece hanging from his neck and a tin cup hung from a wrist with coins deposited there. Another sign on a motionless drumming monkey, 'Needs batteries.'

"Not like this LEG," I replied squashing my ability to look at him with eyes that did glow light, as laser shot from my pupils and fried this arrogant Earth Mannie to a French Fry.

Instead, the man slapped my head again so tears of pain not laser lights came forth from my eyes and nervous gas escaped below.

"What gives with this stinky alien?" He asked, well the alien was afraid, he was amongst humans that are usually in glass beakers in the science class not living free on the range.

"Leave it Ryan," the leg owner and when he lifted his hand to slap again to show his independence, the girl grabbed his hand and flipped him.

Somersaulted yes, he did land flat on his face. Oh, bet that hurt more than my slaps?

I looked at the leg, IT WAS MY FRIEND.

"LEG," I said stroking it, "FRIEND."

Another slap on me.

Then a dog licked me and went off for fallen burgers and hot dogs.

"Boss general what am I supposed to do?" I shouted at the closing exit door of the flying saucer, the door opened, a little green man appeared with big dark eyes and threw me a mirror.

"Plums," that hurt," as the rubbery mirror bounced off my head.

The girl bent down to pick it up investigating.

As an alien I expected a green forked tongue to come from the mirror with hissing.

"What is the make of your foundation?" Mirror asked the girl.

The human stuff on LEG'S chest poked my face, getting me in the eyes so my vision became fuzzy.

"Here crowd, a mirror, come look, it shows us in all dimensions, **impressive** and makes my face funny," the laughing girl not aware the mirror was digitally taking her measurements, WHAT? Did you expect fire and a purple forked tongue to come out of the mirror and swallow her in one go cooked? This is science fiction and admit does occur.

Why did my general throw me a mirror to answer my question why I had been dumped on a Californian beach, well the answer is in the mirror they threw, **so is a secret.**

I got up and ran to the flying saucer and the doorway opened.

"What am I supposed to do here General?" I asked.

A sigh greeted me, and the exit door shut.

That was rude, cruel and left me feeling all alone, a teddy bear needing back in the warm sheets of your bed reader, safe and cozy.

"Hey, the flying saucer is heating up," a man in the crowd and the crowd followed him back a way, then stopped, they wanted reassurance they were seeing a flying saucer and was not because of smoking the funny socks that was making them have a collective dream.

"Hey that little green man is still standing under the flying saucer," a girl shrieked spreading her alarm I was about to be burnt to crisp by the saucer's hot exhaust.

"I got my mobile," a man.

"Someone save him," a girl.

"You save him," someone with sense.

"Why? We can sell what is left to Area 51," a smart human, the burger seller now with bandaged burnt hands wanting revenge and cash to sooth the pain and buy a new drone. It was the flying saucer's fault he had forgotten he was frying, "We got to catch the little one they left behind," knowing a zoo did pay a lot of money for me.

And I was covered in hot saucer exhaust, radiation so glowed and my innards showed as in an X-ray.

"Owe," a unified sound from the beautiful people thinking I was about to POOP, blame the X-ray for they could see a pooh in me.

But I was me, and needed my mirror back for the answer to my question, "Why was I getting dumped here?"

"This yours, want to have a look at the mess that flying saucer made of you, want me to phone 111 emergency?" The laughing girl still laughing as smoking funny socks has that effect.

"Ureka," and I tried to snatch the mirror, but the girl waved it about, so my hands landed places a hybrid human was only taught about in classes aboard a mother ship amongst the stars.

A flying saucer that had *'plumed'* off.

"Titter," I tittered, poked, and tried stroking those places flat. Was I an idiot, no, an INNOCENT ALIEN BOY.

"You a pervert or something, hey folks a pervert, come teach this little man what we do to perverts," and she laughed and put my hands back on places so when her friends gathered round, they could see for themselves I was a pervert needing the day lights beating out of me.

"Mummy," I cried as they began to do exactly that.

A surfboard landed on my head.

A hot burger wok followed.

A cheese knife was plunged into my head.

A burger was thrown on my scalp to cook by a burger van owner.

A gun was fired and the bullet in slow motion went through me with a PLOPPING sound.

A sea gull overhead flew down, ate the burger, and left white stuff.

Something in the sand bit me with a claw.

Two fingers from nowhere poked my big black eyes, GAWD that hurt.

And the laughing girl said, "Sorry Mr. Alien, you should be dead?"

I looked in my mirror and screamed.

HYBRID, COMEDY SCIENCE FICTION

I was a giant burnt burger, those idiots in the flying saucer could have at least waited till I was not under the craft to leave.

The Leg was no longer my friend.

"A zombie, I saw that movie, "The walking Dead,' all about zombies," the burger vendor and from a hip pocket took a .22 derringer and fired directly at my head.

Was it he who had shot me earlier?

Always my head, it was beginning to ache.

"That was not funny, why did you do that mister?" The laughing girl not laughing.

"This is America where all carry guns, and he is an alien," the burger vendor in a New York accent giving it away he was an alien, not a native of sunny raisin California.

"Oh dear, not my fault as I gingerly back stepped towards sand dunes as he was set upon by happy people who believed in 'Gun Control.'

"We can make him eat his own raw Chop Suey Burgers," one of the angry beautiful people.

"Yes, with double portion of gherkins," another.

"Here stuff this spatula up somewhere while still hot," another holding the wooden handle, as the other end glowed red.

There was a scream as the vendor begged MERCY.

Well, did the cruel spatula holder do it, *I leave that to your imagination?*

"Hey handsome, you are a hybrid, they are your people, join the party, but better not looking like that, let me tidy you up some," my mirror.

"A hybrid?" So, remembered my biology classes that I came bottom in. A hybrid was a cross between a tiger and a lion and was infertile. "EEK," I shrieked and had to have a look at places and sighed, I had what it takes.

"What are you looking at 'Four Eyes,' and you better get some new glasses as your pair has melted into you. Just why are you not dead, want me to phone emergency?" It was the laughing girl. I looked at her legs, were they friendly or enemy?

They looked nice so must be friendly.

"Friend," I said.

"What you looking at my little alien? Like what you see?" So, she stood there in a Napoleon pose so I tried to swallow, but the roasting had made my throat dry, instead my forked purple tongue limped out at an angle.

See I do have one.

"Hiss."

"Here this will help," and she stuck the smelly sock that was glowing into my mouth, closed my nose, so I breathed.

"Friend, take me to your leader," I said and laughed, then the mirror fed up, disgusted, and annoyed, losing patience glowed so the green lights of the Aurora borealis shone from it.

"Pick me up Mr. Beag," the mirror pleaded with me.

The laughing girl stuck the glowing smelly sock in my mouth again.

I stuck my purple tongue out at the mirror licking leaving smears.

The mirror replied by levitating in front of me and green lights enveloped my body.

"Owe," the girl.

"Owe," her friends.

"Owe, yeh, I must get a butterfly net and capture that little alien, my religious friends will pay me dearly for it, he is a threat to the creationist theory," the burger seller rubbing his hands in anticipation.

GREED had him.

"Owe," me as the green lights electrocuted me.

Fireballs erupted places setting my shorts alight.

The Sand under my feet turned to glass.

My teeth chattered, my eyeballs span, my purple tongue shot licking the owner of LEG giving her electric current.

"Owe," the watchers.

"I got to keep this alien," the owner of LEG tingling, now wanting to take me home and fill a tank with water and stick me in it. She knew aliens had cities under the sea and could breath in water as had gills, she read science fiction and watched films about 'Atlantis.'

"Wow, the little alien is cooking again," she added laughing.

The burger vendor slapped a burger on my head, he did sell it dearly as a genuine 'Alien Burger,' and someone did buy, someone who went to bed nights with a Bud Light Year Soft Toy.

I came to my senses and asked the mirror telepathically for a pain killer.

"No, or you will not learn your lessons," the mirror calming down so was not electrocuted further.

"What lessons, I do not know what I am supposed to do on this planet?" I loudly.

"Make more hybrids and prepare for a change of Earth leadership, you will be these people's leader, it will be easy, perform cheap tricks, tell lies, act rich and you will be their leader by New Year," my mirror lying.

"Slap," from a human hand and, "do not think about it, 'Four Eyes,'" the laughing girl.

I reached out to grab her and hold her prisoner as my human teacher, but because of the melted glasses in my head and burnt hair poking my eyes grabbed what no gentleman should grab, so doubled up with pain as the laughing girl's knees went into operation rhythmically to as 'Good as Hell,' and yes, she was laughing hysterically.

Sand crabs exercised at our feet.

I WAS NOT laughing.

"Mirror," I gasped but silence greeted me.

Mirror, I remembered in a fog was a female electrical spirit, a binary specter invited out of the Dark Matter via The White Noise to inhabit this mirror and be my mentor for this mission.

I was to be a rabbit and was off to a poor start.

Perhaps visiting a vet. I knew what humans did to animals, the same what we do to alien species we collect throughout the galaxies, control their urges. Yes we aliens have science fiction writers too and our own Area 51.

The vendor took his burger away, "Thirty dollars for a one only, full of green cheese."

"Give me one," the chap under the bowler with the cane.

"Money," the vendor.

And the little man under the bowler gave him a look borrowed from 'Puss and Boots.'

"Get lost buddy," the heartless vendor.

"Here is ten, take it or leave it," and was the funny girl slapping money into the vendor's free hand. "Give me back my hand buster," the girl as the vendor held it with a smirk.

That did it, the laughing girl said, "Ah So Chop," and freed her hand.

"Thank you madam, my first meal all day," the man under the bowler and swirled his cane walking away, using his hat to say 'Bye.'

"I am in love," the beat-up vendor.

[Chapter 2] — Green cheese

Beautiful beach folk

I did like to stuff the vendor full of moon green cheese, but he was lucky I was small and he big and that calmed me down, so I lay on the sand waiting to be put back together by MIRROR.

Let me see, I had been toasted a few times, poisoned by radiation, beat up, and was naked so my human flesh was chilling as the warm sun was still on the horizon, over there and me here.

"Mirror, why am I so small?" But mirror replied giggling and sniggering.

Anyway:

A small black spot suddenly dropped from the sky to bob in the Pacific Ocean and a thousand-dollar drone now on the

waves to be washed onto a beach and a kid looking for dropped valuables did find it, "EUREKA," of course the kid did shout.

"Here," and the laughing girl threw a rug over me and sat beside me.

I recognised what she was drinking from class, a fizzy caramel drink. My alien half dominated as my human half was sending messages that I was thirsty and starving.

So, explains why my purple tongue snatched the caramel drink from the girl.

"Owe," the amazed girl.

"I can save you," the burger vendor waving a chopper and his .22.

"Owe," her friends with many open palms pushed his face away, the gun they stole, his burger van they in and out went with armfuls of sausages, burgers, sesame buns, jars of gherkins, chickens they did find out the hard way were rubber.

They were happy beautiful folk high on the sea air and full of the sounds of nature.

I gave her the empty bottle back.

Then flew into the air before she beat the living daylights out of me.

"I am not smoking smelly socks, you can come back," she waving me down.

"Leg friend," me floating down to her leg.

"Hey, the little alien thinks your leg is you," one of her friends.

"It is," the laughing girl serious now and wiggled toes in front of me, "these are five little piggies."

That confused me as piggies were farm animals and now here in front of me, growing out of her foot, pigs.

"PLUMS," get his mouth off my toes.

I was hungry,

"Pick me up quick," mirror and did, " run."

I saw the burger vendor approaching with a big gun so even the beautiful people scampered, but not LEG.

"BOOM," and a rush of stringing pellets engulfed me.

"BOOM," a second time and was not engulfed in anything but heard screeching and calls for someone's mummy.

I looked back, it was Leg somersaulting the burger seller into the air and using the big gun as a bat as he fell.

"Oh dear," it seemed so painful but still stared.

"Now let me heal you," my mirror and was electrocuted again.

"Hey little alien, you look human," it was Leg, but Leg spoke through lips and a mouth.

"Listen stupid," my mirror and in a second educated me.

"LEG belongs to you, FRIEND?" I asked.

"I am going to be sick," my mirror and mirror understood why they sent me, because I had come bottom of my class. An expendable, someone so silly the humans did see no evil in, no intention of becoming their leader, and because of that, I might succeed.

If not, there was always Area 51 and dissection.

"What is your name my little alien?" The girl who was Leg.

"Beag," I answered smiling.

"What does it mean?" Everyone except the vendor out for the count and when he awoke a dentist needed.

"Small," and I smiled showing ivory teeth, and the teeth were the whitest ever seen so sparkled as stars as aliens kept their gold as filings there.

"Owe," then, "cannot see a thing, close his mouth Dorothy, please," some in the crowd.

"Dorothy," I repeated slowly like an idiot, "not Leg?"

"Yes, Dorothy," and she led me away in red shoes followed by her friends to a pink campervan.

"Rabbit now," I asked remembering my mission.

"It needs a vet," one in the crowd.

"You cannot be serious going in there alone with E.T. after what it said? Another.

"It had a purple tongue, think what it has below, tentacles, suckers," another.

And Dorothy looked and turned me about so all could view a little naked alien.

"EEK, **that** wants to hump," someone.

"Give it your leg Dorothy," another laughing.

"Give it to me," the vendor with gaps in his teeth adding, "I am no longer in love with this horrid girl."

There was the sound of a purple tongue reaching out slapping his face, poking eyes, jabbing throat so he gasped for breath, and then the tongue undid his belt and pulled down his trousers, and no not his shorts.

I had some long tongue and was part of my alien make up, I was a HYBRID.

"Owe," the crowd.

"That was something, think he can do that to my headmistress?" Someone.

"To my dad," another.

"To the school bully," another.

"To my boss," another.

"To my bank manager," another.

It was obvious I had scored.

"My hero," my sarcastic mirror.

WHAT DO YOU THINK LISTENER ABOUT MIRROR?

*

A small dog ran to me barking then jumped me sniffing so I fell over.

The dog's tongue licked my mouth seeking food.

This was Planet Earth so remembering my mission to make friends, I licked the inside of the dog's mouth with my purple tongue.

There ensued a tug of war to get my tongue back.

"Leave it Jack," Dorothy picking the dog up and carrying it away and my tongue rolled away from it.

Dorothy only noticed my tongue as she put the dog down and the dog pulled on it.

"Argh," alien sounds of heaven, sarcasm folks, the opposite.

"Jack, bad boy," and Dorothy tugged my tongue free that span about wrapping itself about her, I admit a few seconds too long, enough for Dorothy to twig and, "Your tongue ever comes near me again chop understand?" Dorothy waving a middle finger.

A sign of greeting so I gave a middle finger back smiling. My mission was to make friends.

I recognised it as a cat from lessons, "Meow," I started chatting to it.

"You speak to animals, why not Jack back there?" Dorothy.

I opened my mouth and rolled out my purple tongue, unnecessary meters of it to impress.

Quickly Dorothy turned green, my tongue had been inside Jack's mouth, what had it been eating, what was sticking to my beautiful piece of anatomy I even had given it a name, "Tongue."

Something moved, a creepy crawly now escaped from the contents of Jack's mouth.

With the end of my forked tongue, I gently caught it, a fly and my forked tongue is like a cats paw, it has a thumb, so held it out to Dorothy with sad tearful eyes.

"A gift for you Earthling woman, LEG," I knew presents were the way to peace.

She did not seem pleased with my buzzing gift.

I tried a sheepish grin and put on pleading eyes.

Dorothy melted and opened a window and my tongue put the bug out.

I waved goodbye.

Dorothy closed the window and patted my head.

I sniffed and let a tear blob run down her leg.

She did not beat the daylights out of me.

Thank the Celestial Beings.

"What a kind whatever you are Beag?" She said and with a Cheshire grin I leaned against her leg more than necessary, I was winning, I knew I was cute.

Then she threw me away like a rag doll.

She had looked in the reflection of the closed mirror and saw me on LEG.

Can an alien have no privacy?

Must I always get the daylights beat out of me?

What gives with Earth girls?

"Hiss," it was the cat, recognizing her mistress was annoyed with me copied suit, "Argh," I moaned as feline talons clawed my nakedness.

"Mirror," I pleaded.

Mirror went in front of the cat and showed an image of a ferocious zoo beast. Well, the cat hissed and went berserk on the nearest handy stress dummy, me.

"Argh," I moaned as the beast ran away, then came back, and lifted its tail and squirted scent on me.

"Plums," I complained.

*

The inside of the camper was the opposite to the spacecraft I had been on, they were hygienically clean. Robot cleaning droids outnumbered us aliens. Every alien had one following waiting for a chance to clean. They were bored, full of Ai, wanting more in their electrical life than cleaning.

I am sure they wanted to be like lesser evolved aliens like humans, able to be anti social.

"Beware humans of those battery-operated monkeys beating cymbals and drums, they might be bored and want to change places with YOU.

The human Leg Dorothy quickly started picking stuff off the floor and pushing whatever into drawers.

In an instant I told mirror to help.

In an instant I learned my mirror was female.

In an instant I was helping as mirror gave me orders where things went.

Dorothy now leaned against a wall next to mirror.

I learned much that socks covered your bare feet so took a pair.

I learned what orange unmentionables were for so put one on.

I did not need what is called a bra but saw Dorothy had one

on, so put one on.

Then found tights fitted me as they stretched up my legs and yes, did laser the lower feet of the red tights. That left feet in socks needing covered so Dorothy, "Try these," and handed me a small pair of stilettos.

With laser beams from the end of my fingers I cut a jean down to size at the legs and mirror was the seamstress to alter the waist, or better be taken to a department store and buy clothes, so handing back the wrecked jeans to Dorothy who was grateful for she said, "Thank you Beag, I always wanted shorts."

Dorothy was also wondering what wonders I still hid. Could speak to animals, my fingers were lasers, my tongue was male and needed watched, yes, I was a wonder.

Then threw a lime shawl over my shoulders and clasped it shut.

A green bonnet she pulled down on my head.

Then opened the camper door and ushered me out.

"Owe," the crowd followed by sniggering.

"A jack ass," the vendor whispering to himself, "a gay alien jack ass," he added thinking of ways to trap me. "Eureka," he shouted that drew attention to himself.

"Hey, the burger seller is still here, I am hungry," and takes one so any evil plans the vendor had cooking changed to cooking burgers and chili refried beans.

"I will dress in alluring woman stuff and lure the alien behind my burger Van where I will use my heavy frying wok on his head, then tie him up with Scots sticky tape, then stuff him in a black bin bag, tie it at the top, and throw it into my small freezer.

Yes, I did need to empty what I have in the freezer, that alien is not that small.

Then off to Area 51 and riches," the vendor and laughed evilly, and because he was laughing dropped a frying burger onto his sandalled feet that sizzled.

Sandalled as this is California the Sunshine State where

raisins are grown and sold for you to eat as full in vitamin C or fermented into watery stuff that these beautiful people soaked the funny socks in and that is why the socks are funny.

"Someone shoot my alien," and was Mirror.

Then Dorothy shut the camper door.

I was alone facing a wall of expectant human aliens waiting for me to juggle firebrands, swallow venomous snakes, swallow piranhas, some chance.

I forgot I had mirror, remembering she was a girl I did need to ask her nicely to do those things to amuse the crowd.

What were these humans expecting, and it dawned upon me, I stuck out my purple tongue and licked faces, just like I seen dogs do in my human behaviour classes.

"Yuck," and one made to grab my tongue.

"Blooming pervert," another.

"Yeh, just look at the way it dresses," another.

"Got an empty bra on too," the consensus and looked pulling it then letting it go.

SLAP," loudly.

"Ugh," that was cruel.

"Hey little alien, I will help you," and was a whisper and looked, and there was a strange looking woman who needed a shave, on the legs and face. She also smelt of burgers.

About turn and "Dorothy let me in," I shouted as I banged on the camper door.

The door eventually opened.

Was this Leg standing in front of me.

A changed LEG.

See was threatening all.

Dorothy was in a dark suit with a hat and dark glasses.

She quickly flashed a badge and threw me into the camper.

"Owe," the crowd as they heard me THUD.

"They going to dissect the little thing," one.

"It was kind of cute," another.

"Do we phone animal protection?"

And the burger vendor scratching his unshaven legs added, "CIA, how do I get that alien away from her, yes, that is the answer, she is a HER," so tore of his female clothes so someone shouted, "Look a pervert."

"Let us beat the day lights out of It," another as they had run out of smelly socks to smoke so wanted to take their anger out on HIM.

So beat the day lights out of him, finished frying the burgers, ate the chopped tomatoes, salads, and sesame buns, emptied the ketchup bottles, and left.

Leaving I.O.U. nothings.

"Never did like him anyway," a satisfied eater.

"Yes, his legs needed shaved," another wiping mustard on the moon of a passing folk unnoticed.

"It was the beady eyes," another belching.

"Hey, you wiped your dirty mustard hands on my moons?" And the girl in a bikini had a seven dan so beat the PLUMS out of that man.

And a camper van whose wheels were designed to transverse sand or snow drove away into the rising sun.

Pelicans swooped down attracted by the burger smells.

"We are out of here," the crowd.

"What about me?" A squeaky voice from a burger vendor.

"Never heard anyone," the common reply.

He over charged his under cooked or burnt burgers. His cooking area heaved roaches, baby flies, and not all things were kept in a freezer, freezers cost money to run.

Soon those who beat the PLUMS out of him left I.O.U.'s, nothings, did be holding their tummies seeking latrines, and since were out in the dunes, the dunes, then Emergency as probably had dysentery.

*

And Beag was not told to wear a seat belt as was not necessary aboard a ship that could make an abrupt turn or come to a stop at five thousand miles an hour with the occupants still being normal, and why Beag did not wear one, do you?

So, explains why Beag was thrown all over the inside of the camper, so messed the place up.

"Meow," yes there was a cat to blame.

"Woof," yes, a dog to blame.

"This will do," Dorothy halting the camper outside a lonely phone both looking over San Diego Bay, and "PLUMS," a scream of horror and yes, the cat and dog were blamed for fighting making a mess of her camper.

I just sat levitating sucking thumb.

All the cleaning work Beag put in was undone. "Get out," and the camper door was opened, and the pets encouraged out with fresh air smells.

Beag went too until Dorothy realised the alien stays no matter how messy he was.

He just needed house trained, and she asked, "Is he potty trained?"

*

Smells they knew, that means they were home, yes, overlooking naval dockyards, city innards, and the smells of morning coffee and doughnuts, and knew where to go.

A popular vendor's who sold such delights to the early morning workers.

"Here Diego, it is me Ronaldo, let me in," Diego heard scratching at the handy back door of his coffee vendor business.

"Sweet Jesus, a person who has had a bad sex change come to rob me," and Diego slammed the door shut on his first cousin who had been overhauled so much was no longer recognizable as he was the vendor who earlier had used a .22 derringer, fried burgers on Beag's head and fallen in and out of love with Dorothy and had the day lights beaten out of him often so only darkness remained in his thoughts.

The seven deadly sins had him.

"Sweet Jesus nothing," Ronaldo mumbled with the handy

Back door pressed against his nose, his lips too, yes them too.

Ronaldo felt the handy back door open, and a wet mop pushed into his face, so he fell backwards. Not to worry, there was lots of sand and prickly nettles for Ronaldo to fall onto.

See we know how to take care of bad guys in this tale.

"Hey, you are Ronaldo," Diego looking though Ronaldo's wallet and identification.

Was Diego robbing his first cousin.

To the spoils the victor so YES.

Could he get away with this crime, Ronaldo was at his feet.

Or was he seeking identification of the clown at his feet for Ranaldo had been roughed up so much he no longer looked human, he looked himself so was the opposite of good looking.

That is a more positive outlook.

And Ronaldo held up a frightening hand to choke the left kneecap of Diego.

Diego with, "Ah So," swatted the hand away.

"What do you want cousin?" For Ronaldo was full of quick rich schemes that needed your cash inflows with no returns.

"It so secretive I cannot tell you out here, take me in so I can clean up and have breakfast," Ronaldo and there he was, wanting a freebie coffee, a dozen waffles with maple syrup, scrambled egg, and your Sunday Best clothes.

And Diego picked Ronaldo up and whispered, "This had better be good or Ah So Chop."

"I know where E.T. is, help me catch it and be mega rich," Ronaldo before Diego in a fit of laughter used Ronaldo's head as a basketball.

Did that mean Diego did not believe Ronaldo his first cousin?

Does that explain why he used Ronaldo's head as a basketball?

That means Diego was a bigger muscular man, yes it does.

And he was in hysterics and so were his hands so what he held was in hysterics also, that meant the basketball moaned as it bounced from left to right hand and Diego thought this hysterical.

He obviously held Ronaldo in low esteem.

Was Diego being mean because his brain had heard, "and be mega rich," no "we will be mega rich." Did Diego understand those words or was he just a big man who ate Whey Protein in front of a long mirror flexing muscles asking the mirror, "Are my biceps not the biggest in the land?" Of course, mirror replied thinking and Diego liked it that way.

Anyway, did Ronaldo whisper what he knew, or did he imagine he did, let us face it, he was looking like a clown and after that door shut in his face?

Oh, messy it was, a tooth dangled from his nose from the end of a long bogie.

Would you tell Diego the truth after that or plan REVENGE.

So, let us look at whose having breakfast in Diego's eatery who might have eves dropped?

The Three stooges, yes, extras for a remake of the 'Stooges Life.' Now all sitting in each others chairs as had jumped off and on so quick not to be noticed doing so, so now Boss Stooge, Mo was slapping heads for order and not to mention why had they left their seats, 1] to get slapped by Mr. Mo, 2] to use the latrine that was a septic tank and needed emptied, so wise customers waited till they paid the bill and ran behind a cacti outside, 3]

to take advantage that Diego was busy playing basketball with Ronaldo to stuff their mouths full of what treats was on display on the counter without paying. Give them twenty minutes and they did need a cacti each, so why eat here, the next eatery was FAR AWAY down the interstate and those strawberry cream doughnuts sang to you, "EAT ME PLEASE EAT ME," or was it to eves drop as The Stooges were curious children in adult clothes.

Did you eves drop reader?

Now a hardened man whose shoulder holster had showed jumping in and out of the swivel chair in the breakfast diner pretended not to notice the Stooges and when Larry reached to steal his bacon and egg roll this man stuck it and the hand in his big mouth and looked at Larry.

Larry gulped and slowly withdrew his hand and the mouth closed on an empty roll.

Why had this tough man left his seat, spilling his silver handled pistol on the linoleum floor, to eves drop.

The safety was off, the pistol went off and the bullet zinged by Curly Joe, hit a stuffed moose, and bounced back singing Mo's scalp and then fell limply on Curly's lap.

Mo slapped him good; the bullet was his fault.

Did you eves drop reader?

And retrieving the pistol was a good excuse to leave his seat and rip where he sits as he deliberately wore sizes to small to emphasise the muscular bulges under the cloth.

He was a tough He Man that is why.

Now a luscious red head as the script demands a luscious woman who had torn her stockings getting off and, on the swivel, chair so quickly smiled at him sharing that embarrassment.

Why had she left her seat to ladder her stockings, to eves drop.

The stockings were an excuse to get off the swivel seat, stretch and show the room what she was packing, she was packing herself, it was Dorothy, LEG.

And if you were not ogling the stockings, did you eves drop reader?

Now a delivery driver who had finished his night run had stuffed the whole egg roll into his mouth to look natural that he had not left his swivel chair at the breakfast diner. Why had he left his seat, to cough up the whole egg roll he had stupidly stuffed in his mouth onto Mo, no, to eves drop.

It was that or keep using his fingers to get the big egg roll out of his mouth with his grubby fingers as he was going blue.

Joining Curly Joe and Larry eat off Mo his egg roll was his excuse to leave his swivel seat.

Did you eves drop too reader?

Dorothy's dog liked coffee so was slurping his spilt drink. He did not mind; he was eves leaning on the Three Stooges to learn what they had eves dropped.

And a Blonde girl as is said, 'Gentlemen Prefer Blondes,' so we got one here, and who is she, a blonde girl with a suitcase she had flicked open in a hurry getting on and off her swivel chair

and Dorothy's cat was now inside it for cats are quick. Why had she left her seat, to get Dorothy's cat out of her suitcase where a pillow, sleeping bag and thermal elastics were being shredded as cats need to claw as is a cat thing, no, it was to eves drop.

So, who she is can be explained as the tale unfolds, a hint is the black eye stuff girls use has run down her cheeks as she has been crying. Maybe she was Mrs. Adams double and never needed so is hitting the road.

Crying, why?

She never got to sing the Addams Theme song, 'Addams Groove.' What codswallop, she is crying, no, it is that black gooey stuff on her eyes.

Did you throw her out because she could not pay her share of the rent as she lost her part in a local theatre production of 'Skrek The Musical' as she complained to much the granny wolf suit was too hot under the theatre lights.

Who is she?

Mind your business, **it is a secret for just now.**

And did you eves drop or were too busy admiring her thermal elastics?

The thing is, why did all these people leave their swivel chairs and where did they go?

Now is the time to end your suspense.

They bunched behind Diego at the latrine door holding their breathes going blue.

Perhaps they did not like breathing deeply latrine pongs escaping from a full septic tank?

HYBRID, COMEDY SCIENCE FICTION

That proves they were needing expensive psychiatric help, not the Three Stooges as they were the free psychiatric help.

Then what happened, read on to find out **free**.

Did Mo provide the cheap help by slapping?

It looks like toilet roll is unrolled to the tall man with the pistol.

Was the loo paper stuck to his ankles.

More importantly, was the loo paper clean?

Did he remember to wash his hands?

Do you wash your hands after a dump?

And the paper flowed to the kicked open newspaper stand as whoever was in such a hurry to act normal buying one did not have ten cents so beat the newspaper holder open. It took three men to beat the day lights out of the news paper stand. Well, look at the stooges, three men, reading one newspaper shared between three, with cut out holes where their eyes could watch you unnoticed.

Free newspapers as these stunt men extras were waiting for the remake of the film, 'The Three Stooges.' So did not have money these best friends reading a newspaper upside down.

Anyway, "Jesus, who let a Tasmanian devil in here?" Diego coming in through the kitchen.

And they all pointed at a dog.

"Out and to think I feed you," Diego waving hands and arms at the dog.

Did we forget to mention that Dorothy's dog was a Jack Russel SO DRAGGED Diego out and played rough with him as his personal Frisby.

Leaving those inside to stare at each other and sometimes Mr. Mo slapped his two friends as needed slapped.

"Meow," and who did let the cat out?

You, the animal lover?

It got itself out as cats have razors as claws, so all here attracted to the suitcase being opened and saw Miss Freckles

30

jumping out trailing a line of lingerie behind.

The men with imagination looked at the blonde.

Sons of Adam they be.

The Red Head looked at the men accusing them of, 'What are you looking at, never seen elastics?'

But they all had something in common, had they not, they had left their swivel chairs, and the proof is that the empty swivel chairs had been swivelling, EMPTY.

Now the occupants were back in each others' chairs drinking someone else's coffee, finishing eating the doughnut, the scrambled eggs, the gherkins, and knew it and ate to prove they had never left their swivel chairs hoping they did not need emergency.

Do you go about restaurants quickly sitting down finishing off what was left when a customer leaves from table? Students do, see what I mean?

And Diego returned covered in sand, poop careless whatever has had dropped, dog saliva and dropped ice cream.

Remember he had been playing with a Jack Russel.

He needed the lavatory.

Would he notice there was no loo roll left?

And 'ENGAGED' was on.

"Tra a La," he heard Ronaldo singing brushing his teeth.

Diego knew it was his toothbrush being used.

Diego went mental and tried beating the door down.

He needed a pee and dump and then he noticed the trail of loo paper to the tall man.

Diego gritted teeth and advanced with hands in a throttling mood.

The man flipped open his jacket, bulb light flashed off the silver handle.

Poor Diego was exhausted after the Jack Russel had used him as a frisbee.

Not a "Ha So," escaped Diego who went back to the eatery.

Eyes followed him.

All thought the same, 'Is he dumping in the freezer? If he does not wash and change, I am eating else where,' but was lies as the nearest eatery was miles down the road near San Diego. It is called collective thought and, in the future, if future willed, they did be back and today forgotten.

But today was not to be forgotten.

Dorothy left and re-entered.

The men smiled.

You know why, they were oglers.

A small creature ran between her legs, it was Jack her Jack Russel.

Then a bigger creature entered, it looked like an ill cross-dresser as still wore what Dorothy had stuffed Beag into.

SILENCE.

The men no longer smiled, gagging sounds instead, Beag was sired by ugliness.

"It is true," then slapping sounds.

The eaters went back to reading the newspapers upside down watching Beag through the holes in the newspaper and the cat brought the lingerie to Dorothy expecting a rewarding cuddle.

The blonde got up and retrieved the washing and smiled at Dorothy, then looked down at Beag longer than usual.

"Hello cutie, I am Susanna Lou," and stuffed chewed gum into Beag's mouth and a calling card, "Exotic dancer for parties," and walked away.

"LEG," Beag and reached out to touch the departing calf muscle.

A slap descended on him.

Dorothy was training.

"Owe," Beag was confused, this planet had legs everywhere.

Then Mr. Mo came over, "What a nice son you have," and patted Beag and stuck a badly chewed cigar into Beag's mouth. Of course, his friends tried to tell Mr. Mo boys do not smoke

cigars so where slapped.
    Mo lit the cigar.
    Beag ate the cigar.
        There was an amazed silence.
        Out of habit Mr. Mo slapped Beag and saw a clenched fist coming his way, YES connected, and Mr. Mo managed to keep

the gem from the ring in his mouth, Dorothy was after all in black wearing black glasses **so saw nothing.**
    CIA on a badge on her right heaving bosom.
    Mr. Mo's friends kept staring there as they hauled Mo back to his swivel seat.
    The jewel did pay their breakfast.
        Then the man with the shoulder holster used his eyes to check Dorothy over and especially Beag, so the man nodded satisfaction, then twirled so his shoulder holster showed.
        "Hi, I am McSweeny," and stuffed a calling card down Dorothy's chest suit pocket.
            Why did McSweeny twirl, The Lord knows as I do not, perhaps the mysterious alure of Dorothy in all that black freaked him out, or perhaps he was once a ballerina, or an idiot, *which do you prefer?*
        And "No one paws my boobs uninvited mister," Dorothy seconds before she put her knee somewhere.
        McSweeny did get back to his swivel chair where he buried his face in his hands, where he complained, "This breakfast is cold, I am not paying," but was hiding the pain in his hands.
        He was McSweeny, tougher than 'Die Hard' and villainous girls could beat the day lights out of him to find out what he had eves dropped and he did laugh, yes, Mr. Tough Guy.
        "I am here to collect a package, oh this must be it," the delivery driver spitting egg over Dorothy as he reached to pick

up Beag, and a girl with twenty Dans does not take kindly having chewed egg roll with saliva clinging to it spat on her, perhaps a bogyman as well?

Yes, you guessed correctly as with one aimed kick sent the delivery driver up to the ceiling fan where he rotated a while then fell off exactly into his swivel chair,

Dorothy walked over to the eatery.

"A child's breakfast for one, and scrambled eggs for me, a bacon rasher for Jack and a bowl of cream for Freckles, Diego, after you have washed," Dorothy added to sighs of relief.

No one wanted to travel miles down Interstate 5 to a new eatery needing a latrine.

All eyes looked at Diego.

Diego looked at the loo.

The loo door opened, and Ronaldo exposed.

"Owe," the eaters as Ronaldo had done a bad job cleaning himself up. Why he had cauliflower ears, a swollen red nose, bust lips, black eyes, ripped clothes as was waiting for Diego hand outs.

"Are you a LEG?" Beag asked looking at Ronaldo's hairy knees and made cringing disapproving sounds. These legs were not worthy of worship, firstly they needed shaved, secondly, they were knobbly.

"A LEG?" The eaters repeated looking at each other thinking aliens referred to themselves as LEGS.

And Ronaldo snatched Beag and ran out the handy back door.

See Diego was correct about Ronaldo, he was a no-good thieving rascal.

WHAT NEXT?

CHAPTER 3 – SAUCER COMAND

Is this what happens next to Beag, sort of.

An alien dressed in a pressed uniform sat at the end of a long table longer than a certain leader we know uses.

His uniform comprised of an orange sash adorned with medals across his chest. A chest full of glued on chest hair as these green aliens were hairless.

Why the chest hairs, here was an alien Son of Adam.

There was a medal of stars in the middle of the sash acting as a pin. It held him together, no, of course not, it pinned a picture of grinning him there.

That explains a lot about him.

He liked to grin.

His chair was also on a platform so this E.T. was higher than the subordinates seated at the long table that sloped making those approaching him climb. A tricky thing for a waiter as being a slope much spillage occurred to make the slope a place of spillage. What did this uniformed alien do with sloppy waiters, well of course he shouted, "Off with their heads."

He was the typical green alien with big black eyes out of Roswell Area 51.

Shark eyes.

At the table others just like him but smaller or they did stuff him down a waste chute

Also, others not like him but E.T.s. straight out of a Disney Wardrobe.

Imagination time.

And a waiter brought in a dish of sizzling roasts.

Hey, wait a moment, we are told aliens have no mouths or wear no clothes.

And the important alien's mouth moved where a mouth should be, on his stomach, no, the bum, no, the end of the 'willy,' no, just where a mouth should be on a face.

Whoever told us aliens did not have mouths?

It was the government controlling area 51 that is who.

Everything has the food go in one end and exit somewhere far below. Even The Lord Jesus said so.

"Another fine roast Wayne, think is your last cooked meal for us here aboard ship, we all thank you Wayne, what is for desert?" The important alien and the other seated aliens looked at Wayne knowing he did have cooked something wonderful, pancakes in Maple syrup, a giant chocolate cake and an earth girl jumps out the top giggling.

These were aliens.

"General, vanilla soft ice cream covered in chocolate with banana ears, strawberry eyes, and says, 'Take me to your leader,'" Wayne replied bowing, happy he was going back to Earth away from this greedy alien but of course Wayne never said that.

"Sounds nice, but not as nice as you baked as a Baked Alaska Wayne, wheeled out aflame, yes, your last service to us," the general alien making biting sounds, then a yellow tongue came out, wrapped About Wayne, then licked his black lips.

These were aliens.

Wayne was horrified, he looked up, seeking a place of exit, but there was none, only menacing armed E.T.s. licking their lips with coloured tongues. Some rubbing their bellies.

"Oh Lord Jesus save me," Wayne begged in a desperate

prayer.

The room was silent.

"Only joking Wayne, which is what you taught us, humour," and the aliens had a jolly laugh.

Wayne tittered and hoped none did notice he had peed a little, well, not a little, a great pool of frightened wee.

He needed a change of underwear, chef trousers, socks, and shoes.

The general sighed, stood, came, and helped Wayne up, and sent him on his way to get changed. "See you later Wayne," and fluttered his eyes.

"Gulp," Wayne who had not even kissed an earth girl yet.

"Lighten up Wayne, only joking," the general and laughed so he bobbed.

His subordinates laughed too.

And Wayne was full of apprehension, would the general see him later a silver platter a sizzling roast or in swim wear wrestling a giant alien eating octopus in a mud pool.

Poor Wayne and thought the general's line of jokes rubbish.

These were aliens, do you trust them?

This is the secret why Americans carry guns; they know the neighbour is an alien under a rubber human skin sweating to death.

Anyway: "We will send him to help Beag, after all, Wayne is a human sort of, Beag came last in class and Wayne last in cooking, we cannot lose, and send in the cleaners to mop Wayne's fluid up," the general and looked at a wall map, a red blinking light was a BLINKING red marker and next to Beag.

"Beag," was stitched in white on a black flag attached to the blinking red light.

Alien technology was advanced, nothing was being left to chance.

Now another red marker appeared next to Beag's, it had

Wayne stitched on the black flag, its blinking was waiting to be activated, that would happen when Wayne was sent to Beag.

Yes, the mission to repopulate earth with hybrids and take over Earth leadership looked hopeful, Beag was last in his class so could be blamed if caught as an escaped alien from an alien mental health hospital and not from the general his boss , and Wayne was an imaginative cook who could cook their way out of any situation.

The alien general laughed over his two heroes, he thought it a real joke sending these two amongst the humans and smiled over his detailed planning to conquer Planet Earth.

Nothing could go wrong.

It already had, Beag had met a leg he believed was the leader of Earth and it belonged to Dorothy.

"What a LEG," Beag thought as was at that age where a boys room begins to smell strange.

And Wayne was sent to the last known position of Beag, just like that now three people sitting upfront in Ronaldo's pickup in a flash of BLINDING light.

"GAWD I AM BLIND," so Ronaldo swerved on Interstate 5 forcing two Highway Patrol folks on their motorcycles off the road, through the crash barrier so they rode their polished motorcycles first in the air, then down a cliff to the beach below.

"PLUM," and similar words escaped them, probably brown stains places as well from eating too many PLUMS?

Above them a tourist bus full of South Koreans whose driver decided not to collide with Ronaldo's pick up in the middle of the road, *he wanted to live,* so swerved and followed the police officers to the beach. *"Hey driver, what about the safety of your passengers?"*

"Argh," the drivers reply.

Fulminated Stuff in Korean.

We know driver you would do the same to avoid a deer on the road.

Anyway.

An empty eatery as Diego found family ties ended with mega cash rewards for the folk that handed the alien to Fox News.

"Where has everyone gone?" Diego asking himself as was slow and ten minutes later, "Eureka, they all went after Ronaldo," as light illuminated the cook's brain, "So why am I here and they are out there?"

Good question cook, told you he was slow, and those who are slow reading this tale can affiliate with him.

Then the latrine door opened, whoever needed it we can excuse as must have been bursting with number one and two.

"Oh, hello beautiful red headed lady," for Diego was a charmer, "I am in a hurry so can only sell you prepacked egg rolls," as Diego was a salesman to the end. "Er, you not like scrambled egg rolls and was that you screaming, if you want to cry on my shoulder go ahead," as Diego thought women easy, advice is, stop mentioning egg rolls.

"Argh," Diego beginning to look like Ronaldo with swollen ears, black eyes and bust lips and missing teeth.

Then Dorothy was gone.

The sound of a vehicle driving away.

Why did she plaster Diego, she remembered him, his greasy burgers, the colic she suffered, the overflowing latrine, put it simply, well she just did not like him.

Would you like this guy?

"What a woman, I must marry her, what strength, what bosom," for Diego was a sex fiend. "I am coming Ronaldo," and threw away his cook's apron stuffed with rubber chickens and picked up a bazooka, not shotgun. "This is heavy so threw it aside and it was loaded and went off.

The first casualty of looking for Beag was the eatery going up in flames.

Burning rubber chickens rained down.

"PLUM," my clothes are burning so he stripped running out of the demolished eatery and jumped into his 4 x 4 in his crocodile print Y Fronts and lucky for him he kept the keys hanging on a hock in the eatery kitchen in case Hells Angels drove by and stole his bright green 4 x 4 pick up.

Unlucky for Diego who had to wait for the fire engine to arrive from San Diego and by the time it got here the eatery was ash.

"Well, nothing we can do here son," the Chief Fire Officer under a white helmet. "Here better sit in the fire engine and get an oxygen mask on and use some paper hankies to wipe the soot off your face."

And Diego got in and saw KEYS in the fire engine vehicle ignition. He knew Ronaldo had the alien, and he wanted the alien, Ronaldo was always the untrusty cousin handed over to Immigration.

Temptation got the better of Diego.

He also wanted to marry Dorothy and be an American citizen.

"Thief, get him boys," the Chief Fire Officer but Diego had never driven such a heavy vehicle, so the fire officers jumped here and there to escape being run over.

And Diego by luck saw flashing lights at the scene of an accident so headed down Inter State 5 to that.

"I always wanted to drive a fire truck as a kid," Diego looking about for the foghorn and siren.

"Hey buddy, let me in," from a brave fire officer clinging to the door handle, and Diego got such a fright he drove onto the edge where rough grass, cacti, rattlers, and gophers lived.

"My moon," the fire officer shouting letting go of the door handle to pull off angry biting gophers and when they were gone, the cacti thorns, but he never had that opportunity as he blew away into an open top convertible back seat.

"Ouch," he complained as the cacti thorns went places then

added, "Hey a film star and his bawd, it is you, I am right?" And the fire officer turned the drivers head about to have a good look.

The driver was now driving a convertible full of angry gophers attacking his woman.

It was melee.

The film star was no longer steering or looking where to steer.

The car went through the crash barrier with a bump.

The fire officer was bumped out, just as well or he did be blamed and sued. After all the convertible was a 1930 Bentley.

The wig the blond woman used to own, yes used to as shredded by angry gophers cost a lot, more than a fire man's monthly salary as was a designer wig made of the best soft belly mouse fur.

Somebody was going to pay, but not the fire man who had landed on the top of the road watching the convertible hit the beach scattering beach goers.

Hopefully not swashing them.

"Gee, I better clear off," the fire officer tip toing away being smart.

There was no need to tip toe, running did be better.

And Diego drove away using the Foghorn.

This was a hit and run.

Diego faced prison time.

He already did, he was an undocumented immigrant from the Philippines.

He was a wanted man there for driving offences, operating an illegal eatery that food poisoned the locals, having a gun collection without a licence, so was branded a terrorist, yes Diego drive fast.

No concerns there, he was.

*

Did Ronaldo flatten Wayne, I mean one minute the road was empty and the next Wayne there holding his hands to protect his face as Ronaldo swerved his vehicle.

But the general alien back in the mother ship knew when you lost control act as if you are in control, so levitated Wayne and plunked him next to **Beag in the passenger seat.**

Ronaldo did not notice as he was busy making a show, he had his vehicle under control swinging the wheel this way and that as had the mental ability of a peach.

"Argh," he screamed as the vehicle shot off the road into cloudless sky when he noticed Wayne.

"Squawk," a gull and pecked his left ear.

Another cleaned out his nose, gawd that must have hurt. I mean the size of a gull's yellow beak to a human nostril, oh the pain.

Below Highway Police officers hobbled out of the way with beach goers swatting them with picnic baskets for landing amongst them.

"I am going to die, Jesus save me," and Beag did as the little alien knew he was too young to die as well, so using mental powers as his general used, levitated the 4 x 4 back onto the road.

"Owe," from the watchers below.

A lot took mobile pictures.

Soon the levitating half truck did be on the news and Cryptic Alien Programmes, and the Highway Patrol did offer a $5000 reward for information leading to the capture of the dangerous driver of that 4 x 4.

Ronaldo drive fast.

They blew up the image, do you look ugly with that look of terror on you.

Ronaldo looked at last in his mirror.

"Who the hell are they?" He asked driving the vehicle in front of an approaching Church Choir outing flooding the road with hymns.

That explains the horrified screams as the bus drove off Interstate 5 to the soft sand below and a crowd of excited onlookers with mobile phone cameras.

Ronaldo was becoming well known.

Now his history as a bad boy in the Philippines was aired. He was always expelled from school, he skipped National Conscription so was now hated by The American Legion Veterans, the church knew him as 'The Collection Robber,' and that is self explanatory.

He was getting film star status.

There was also a lot of selfies being taken amongst the wreckage.

Never mind, Beag levitated the bus to land softy.

Beag was a sweet good little alien not like the one from, 'Predator,' or 'Alien' series.

And Ronaldo investigated Beag's eyes and saw heavenly clouds where angels played harps, and felt he was a heel, then noticed Wayne.

"I got two of them," and forgot all about heavenly repentance as little devils sat on his shoulders telling him what he could buy with the reward CNC did pay for these two aliens.

Yes, drive fast Ronaldo as emergency vehicles drove past him on the way to the holes in the crash barriers and a helicopter flew past him.

You can upload your pictures and then takes five minutes to get a following.

Ronaldo drive fast, you are a wanted felon.

And he was as he was a cousin of Diego an undocumented immigrant from the Philippines wanted for printing his own money over there, and was caught as put his face onto the peso notes

What a man?

We must admire his stupidity.

Remember he had the mental ability of a peach. He just never thought things through as his excuse was, "I want."

CHAPTER 4 DOROTHY

Dorothy

"No one twirls in cowboy boots in front of me expecting me to faint.

No one spits the remains of an egg roll on my expensive Foundation.

No one expects a lady to use a latrine after Ronaldo has washed in there first.

No one expects anyone to eat Diego's food if he does not wash hands before cooking.

I am Dorothy and like the black suit and glasses I wear, it gives an air of authority over well, McSweeny, The Stooges, the delivery driver, Diego, Ronaldo, all men.

Now after Ronaldo ran off with Beag I somersaulted in the air ripping my trousers places but was not worried as did not have white elastics on.

But Ronaldo was quicker, he had slammed the eatery door in my face, so I got embedded there.

Smart move Ronaldo, I can respect a man who thinks.

And just as I shook my red curls to show all I am beautiful, the eatery emptied over me.

There was nothing left to do but SCREAM.

Then met Diego coming out the eatery where he kept speaking about egg roll, and trying to hug me and he was quick, pinching my moons so beat the PLUMS out of him as I am an American woman.

And Beag jumped in my camper, and I forgot to look in my mirror before reversing. Would you not stare at the way he was dressed, and I forgot I dressed him.

Mirror signal manoeuvre the Highway code yells. It was only Diego behind me anyway.

Yes, it is believable Dorothy does not like Diego.

And heard him scream under my reversing camper, then I drove away. I knew it was not a hit and run as it was a Diego hit,

then was so relieved hearing sounds, but it was gulls squawking over spilled waste containers not Diego screaming, so put the gas pedal down.

You think she more than dislikes Diego, maybe hate is a better word.

I drove fast as heard Diego shouting, he had a bazooka and to come back and marry him or he did use it on my camper.

Then heard explosions and that is when I looked in my mirror to see what was happening behind me.

I screamed in horror.

I had the whole cast of Shrek in my camper.

So took my hands of the wheel to clutch Freckles and Jack for protection and comfort.

"Lady there are two fire trucks ahead," the blonde shouted throwing elastics she had found in the camper to replace what Freckles had shredded, and the white elastics wrapped about Dorothy's face.

Heaven was being merciful as she could not see the two fire trucks.

Mr. Mo being a man of action slapped his friend's heads till they slapped him back and were so busy slapping never saw the two fire trucks.

Then the Fog Horns.

"I am too young to die," was repeated behind Dorothy often and Freckles jumped behind and clawed the stuffing out of The Stooges as they are the slap stick.

Then Jack jumped over to avoid the two fire trucks and helped Freckles but not The Stooges.

And up-front Dorothy pulled off the white elastics and threw them out the open window, so they blew onto the face of the fireman driving a fire truck.

"Elastics, the girlfriend is here?" Only a man could think such thoughts as his truck crashed the safety barrier and wheels spun air.

"Squawk," a seagull pecking his nose.

Never fear those below were used to vehicles landing amongst them.

Selfies were taken off a grinning fireman with white elastics about his neck.

He was a Son of Adam.

Above a circling sea gull was having fun, when would the next vehicle leave the road?

And Dorothy her black stiletto stuck between the pedal, so her camper went fast.

Would she meet the sea gull that pecked noses?

Ahead of her was McSweeny and a delivery driver.

In front of them Diego.

And why only one fire truck turned up at Diego's eatery.

CHAPTER 5 THE GREAT ESCAPE

"Why are you in my camper?" A realistic question from Dorothy to the cast of Skrek .

"Because of them?" An answer from all jerking thumbs backwards.

"Cops," Dorothy and raked about in her glove compartment for a spare CIA badge.

Just as three speeding black and whites were wanting passed her on the way after a fire truck and 4 by 4. It was a tough time for Dorothy to take her hands off the wheel, but she was a determined woman.

"Found it," and stuck her CIA badge over a bosom.

There was no hissing sound.

"Hey Mo, just like your 'Rice Crispy' badge.

And Dorothy slammed the breaks.

A bad judgment as the cast from Shrek behind now buried her.

"Squawk," a lucky sea gull having three black and whites to chose from now sailing through a crash barrier.

"Get out," Dorothy commanded and that is why the camper door was opened and she was pushed out, ok thrown out that sound better.

Mo got behind the wheel.

"Mo you never took driving lessons," Larry and slapping sounds.

"Let me in," Dorothy pleaded outside and was greeted by the front wheels going over her feet, then the back and exhaust.

The camper stopped.

Dorothy's confidence in being a red head returned.

Then Larry appeared and wiggled his moons till Jack let go with a patch of clothing. Freckles on the end of Larry's arm was shaken off.

The camper drove off.

"PLUM," to think I had the alien and now I got nothing," and walked over to her pets to get them to the side of the road.

She bent down to pick UP Freckle in her split trousers as an R.V. drove by, then it suddenly stopped.

There must be a man at the R.V. wheel, then who knows, we are in liberal times?

A jewelled hand adjusted the side mirror so the driver could get a good ogle.

Jewels flashed in the torch light.

Torch beam?

Yes, the jewel owner held a torch onto his jewelled hand so the gems did sparkle, speak to Dorothy, "I am loaded, be a good red head and a jewel might be yours. There is a pile of dirty plates needing washed, the septic latrine emptied at the next pit stop and, AND?"

A jewelled hand waved her over expecting obedience, it was a long walk to San Diego with pets.

In the caravan side mirror the driver saw the CIA badge. "Just like mine from Coco Pops."

"Hello sweetheart lost, are we?" Yes, he was a man at the wheel. What about the rings, they looked expensive, he had an open shirt showing off a mass of blond curly hairs. The shirt was black, it was contrast.

Oh yeh, the shirt had gold $ print on it.

A gold chain was about his neck advertising money for you if you floss my teeth.

He wore sunglasses.

His face looked familiar.

It was the hair saloons business if you wanted to look like a young Robert Redford. You did for cash for that made the world go round.

He had paid heaps to look like Redford but still looked like Marty Freeman from Frankenstein.

He had decided Dorothy was a 'Material Girl' otherwise she could walk in those, 'Shoes not made for walking.'

The driver blew a pink bubble gum that exploded over his sunglasses and while he was groping to clear them, Dorothy said, "Ha So, government business and had thrown Freckles onto his crotch.

Freckles knew what to do.

There was the zip of talons being exposed, a hiss, spitting and Freckles went to work.

In no time at all the driver jumped off his cushions so he could reach the steering wheel and was out of the driving seat leaping into the R.V. depths.

"Finish him off," Dorothy commanded Jack and the Jack Russel hung onto the man's moons ripping his yellow swim shorts to shreds exposing prints of bikini clad Yogi Bears.
This guy had a sense of humour.

HAD.

In no time Dorothy was beside him and heavily pushed him into the latrine where HE shut and locked the door **by himself** thus vacating ownership of the R.V. to Freckles, sorry, Jack, no, Dorothy who flicked her mass of red hair and from a pocket, a small lavender hair spray.

"If this is a robbery, I have no money, I am a family man on vacation, leave me alone."

She did, she became the new driver.

"Gawd no," she heard the man shout, a hiss, and a bark.

A lot of noise came from the latrine.

In his escape the man had locked the pets in the latrine also.

Pets that knew what to do, to finish the job off.

"No one steals my little alien from me," Dorothy speeding away.

SO:

Ahead a camper zig zagged many times across the road and the following sea gulls had multiplied.

A junkyard of vehicles was building up on the beach with a lot of folks wanting REVENGE.

Did anyone else in the camper have a driving license?

"I do," Curly Jo.

Mo came to a stop by coming off the gas pedal. He had forgotten the brake pedal.

Slap many times, "Why am I driving, change places," and Larry did and "Yippee," hit the gas.

"Oh, Jesus I will become a Methodist Minister if you save me and not them, please," Susanna Lou wanting distance from The Stooges.

And by accident the camper television came on.

"Rewards for," and mentioned a fire truck and a 4 x 4 pick up, $5000 apiece.

"Owe," The Stooges then that changed to Mo, "Who let Larry behind the wheel?" As Larry took his first driving lesson and coming his way a television crew.

"Film this darn it," a director in the television van as it headed for the beach.

"Squawk," many times.

"Gawd, it pecked my nose," a crew girl.

And half a mile up the beach those already on the beach watched. Yes, motorcycle officers, a choir bus, a convertible, many cars and now a van, smoking weed on lonely beaches had ended.

Ronaldo time.
Now Beag was staring at Ronaldo.
That made Wayne stare also, it was better than staring at a road rushing by, but the thing was, Ronaldo felt uneasy with aliens staring at him, especially the human looking one in a chef's outfit.
Aliens ate humans he was told. First chance he had he did turn the tables and eat him.
"I know all about chef outfits and aprons stuffed with rubber chickens for effect, "Ronaldo and wondered if he was about to receive a chopper in the back of his head and an apple in his mouth.
Was he dinner, he was afraid of his captives now. First chance he did murder them both with arsenic poisoning and still claim a reward for showing the world bodies of dead aliens.
Well, if you cannot spend the time, do not commit the crime and choosing arsenic just shows us Ronaldo was THICK as TOAST.
And he was a wanted man and about to be on the F.B.I.'s most wanted list.
Well, the beach friends of Dorothy wanting the rewards had phoned in to chat about an alien visitor and Dorothy had him, and she was driving a camper.
The cat was out of the bag but not really it was in a latrine finishing of an R.V. owner, *some cat it was.*
"So, you are an alien?" Ronaldo watching Beag stroke his hairy leg pinging hairs off.
"LEG," Beag said, and Ronaldo worried some more, "I am a married man with twenty kids," he shouted at Beag.

He should have been watching the road and might have seen the police helicopter in front hovering just above the road ahead.
"Hands up," a voice on a microphone from the helicopter.

" Certainly," the wrong reply.

So not only did Ronaldo not look at the source of the command, but he also held up his hands.

The helicopter did an emergency lift but the 4 x 4 still clipped a running board on the helicopter sending it spinning into a tree, where the occupants dived out and rolled away to the sand below unable to stand as dizzy.

Chipmunks in those trees they had knocked out from eating acorns now clung to them, chipmunks needing counselling after this.

So, the helicopter tumbled down too bursting into flames missing them, like stated, children could read this tale at bedtime so no messy emergency bits.

Too prove it, the chipmunks roasted their acorns in the flames and folks came over and toasted marshmallows and hot dogs. Someone played 'Baby Shark Dance,' and a family atmosphere existed and not one person screamed at the chipmunks, "Look Rats."

"You did that," Wayne pointing a rubber chicken close to Ronaldo's face as all 'World Class Chefs' carry one for an emergency.

"Ouch my right eye, you little PLUM" Ronaldo's exact words so never saw the hot dog vendor ahead swerve off the road.

Those watching saw it and were greedy.

Lucky for all beach watchers now made their way to the hot dog van bouncing down the cliff to the sand below. Lucky all the sleeping Lynx, coyote and tramps that rolled out of their burrows after the van did not bruise the beach folk, why, BECAUSE HOT DOGS WERE AVAILABLE.

"Lovely, pass the American mustard," and "where is the ketchup," and "I want a triple cheeseburger," was heard.

Where these drivers from the eatery of Diego's part of a climate change effort to stop car emissions?

No, they were ordinary folk suddenly presented with a get quick rich scheme, no questions asked, the alien would be handed over to a buyer's back door, which meant no taxes paid either.

Ordinary hungry folk that the warm breeze brought quickly to their olfactory senses the smell of the mysteries of a Hot Dog Van.

AND "I want Dorothy, where are you taking me?" It was Beag in Ronaldo's pick up.

SILENCE as Ronaldo was thick as toast at times remember.

"I do not like you, you are a greasy cook," Wayne recognising one of his own and pressed a finger into Ronaldo's waist.

Bad timing, all that soft eating meant soft belly flab for a finger to sink into, curl about a kidney and flick it.

"Oh Gawd," Ronaldo going faint.

Yes, a troubled time for Wayne to practice butchering skills

as a Sunday preacher with his dog collar showing minding his own business was cleaning his glasses so was a useless driver and explains why he did not need much from Ronaldo to go through the crash barrier and head to the sand below.

"What was that?" Ronaldo acting innocent as a King James black bible flew in the driver's window busting his lips. *It was Divine slapping.*

"I want my Dorothy," Beag and wacked Ronaldo on the head with his unbreakable handy mirror.

Just when a bus load of football players and supporters came his way.

The sounds and squeals of celebrations and bra waving from bus windows turned to frenzied shrieks as they saw the 4 x 4 come straight at them.

Ronaldo shrieked also.

Mirror sank into the depths of mirror.

And Beag levitated himself and Wayne out of the vehicle and headed into the hill bush where mountain lions, coyotes, lynx, racoons, bears, and seagulls squawked.

And just as the bus collided with the 4 x 4 Ronaldo leapt

free.

A wise move.

One of those bras waved from a bus window slapped his face leaving a red welt on his head.

A pair of stilettos got his eyes.

A twelve pack of famous beer hit his head.

A rugby ball was stuffed into his mouth.

Elastics covered his whole head to the neck.

Were they clean? Did the wearers listen to mother and change daily?

A jock strap dangled from his mouth.

It had just come from the game.

Bible pages covered his eyes.

Ronaldo walked away dazed seeing aliens everywhere, trouble was, which where the real ones?

He looked at what he was holding from the bus, a giant sex toy, well it was a football team in celebration.

Ronaldo screamed in horror at what he held and ran, yes, ran into a crash barrier and rolled into boulders, bushes, a sleeping feral cat so was clawed, tried to stand but slipped on a thrown away pizza and zoomed down to the beach while pecked by a thousand sea gulls.

Many got his nose.

He got what he deserved.

The bible pages wafted towards the clouds.

Diego wafted downwards.

"I am not done," he gasped at the bottom when sensible folk did say, "I am done," and breath their last; but he was Ronaldo and knew he had to scramble back the way he came.

Well, he had too, angry folk on beach buggies recognised him as, "that twerp who drove us through the crash barrier," and those police officers amongst them where waving handguns.

"I am an illegal immigrant and face LIFE so I must vamoose," was his good advice to himself.

Thing is, that bus of football players top side was balancing on the crash barrier, yes just above Ronaldo. A swaying bus as those inside where eager to get out.

Soon the roadside was full of half naked bodies.

A bad omen as drivers passing ogled so deserved going through the crash barrier.

Twenty-one cars sailed out.

Is anyone keeping count of the total so far?

"Missed me," Ronaldo making faces at the occupants of the vehicles as they sailed over him to hit the sand, some in the sea splashing suffers off their boards.

And a purple elastic hanging out the back emergency window was blown free by a warm breeze, so the centre of gravity altered in the dangling bus.

And the empty bus rolled upon Ronaldo.

"Jesus," as Ronaldo had been brought up a good Roman Catholic in the Philippines.

And Jesus remembered Ronaldo as the exit door covered him.

"What a mess these college kids leave," was the impression he got from all the tangled clothes and hampers flying about.

That battered him silly.

Was this a Divine warning.

A mess he caused, and The Lord Jesus did not forget that as the bus rolled away and Ronaldo stood there relieved and that is when the spare bus tire landed on him, see, Jesus remembered what a schmuck Ronaldo was.

And that still did not stop this determined man going up the hill.

Bullets zinged into the rubber saving Ronaldo.

Under the crutch.

One pated his hair.

Yes, Our Lord Jesus must have a loving soul, or the Highway Police below were poor shots.

"I want my aliens," Ronaldo getting to the top in record time.

The question is, "His aliens want him?"

Would you like Ronaldo as your friend?

So, Beag looked to Wayne for directions, it was his planet.

And a mountain lion roared, coyotes howled, several lynxes screamed, a bear grunts, racoons laughed, reintroduced wolvers salivated, and vultures circled over Ronaldo.

And Ronaldo noticed and was afraid.

We ask again, did his aliens want him?

They will be all right, they are aliens straight out of the Book of Enoch, so we can leave them to return to those crazy other folk that are driving on Interstate 5.

*

"Got you friend," McSweeny driving fast seeing Ronaldo crossing Interstate 5 towards the bush and wild animals waiting to devour him.

Yes, The Lord was having mercy on Ronaldo.

McSweeny speeded up, "Never liked his fries, gave me colic," as the man with the shoulder holster gritted his teeth and with both hands put on sunglasses.

A no hands on the wheel driver is just asking for trouble and it came as a black saloon car full of men under black felt hats rounded the bend ahead.

In the back seat was a GOD FATHER, a severed plastic horses head was at his feet and the man on the running board was pleading for more time to pay off his loan.

The God Father replied by rubbing his cigar on the man's head, well of course this should have had the effect of the man screaming, holding his head, and bouncing away.

And that is exactly what happened, he bounced away into the bush, lucky for him as McSweeny intent on taking Ronaldo out never saw the Black gangster limousine ahead so ran over him.

And the driver of that limousine was watching the man with the cigar stuck in his head bounce away after meeting

McSweeny.

What a collision.

What a noise.

You mean the bouncing man had met the wildlife, no, the sound of cars meeting, crunching, and the screams of tyres braking hard.

What goes round comes round.

There was no air balloon in the back of the limousine, so the God Father left his seat and flew out the front windscreen.

Horrid it was.

That is Justice American Wild West Style.

And the man bouncing away bounced to the folk below on the beach, "Here bouncing man with a smoking head," and was given a hot dog and a strange cigar that smelled funny, so the bouncing man was happy, see, a child's tale this.

At the last moment McSweeny saw the collision coming and in microseconds using his Seal Training of years past somersaulted out the drivers side.

Lucky for him he was driving an old Mercedes World War 11 black convertible.

How did a man with a shoulder holster afford such a collectors relic?

Was he a good gun man or bad gun man?

That is a secret for just now.

The important thing is he rolled down Ronaldo.

"EEK," Ronaldo.

"I know you are an illegal immigrant, and you know where the little alien is?" McSweeney handcuffing Ronaldo and dragging him into the bush. Using fingers in the nostril method, always subdued the prisoner.

"Did you hear what that cop just said?" One of the mobsters outside the busted limousine.

"Yeh, and think our Boss has had it," a hood answering kicking God Father in the ribs to see if he responded.

The sound of a rib busting.

See, what goes round comes round.

Another opened God Father's eyes wide and poked them for s response.

"Yeh, dead," another slapped God father's face to make sure.

Another stuck a knife places, "Yeh dead."

"What are we waiting for, the car was not insured, let us be off before the Highway Patrol comes, off after those men and

find an alien and be mega rich," the fourth mobster and ran ahead quickly followed by his friends.

Four hoods went after Beag.

"Wait, we got to get rid of the evidence, we got to push the limousine and God Father off the road first," one of them thinking hoods.

Do you think they did kill each other off?

And below, "Owe," from watching folk eating hot dogs in ketchup watching God Father leave the limousine and get pecked a million times by sea gulls, see, Jesus remembered him.

And on a hilltop, "Meow," a mountain lion at Beag's feet and a lynx licked the back of Wayne's head.

"Owe," the pair responded to the accident scene below.

"That is hairy knobbly legs, not like Dorothy," Beag and threw his mirror into the sky where it did an arial ballet.

"Owe," the watchers on the beach.

And McSweeny puffed and panted dragging Ronaldo up the bushy hill by the nostrils. May we ask his subconscious, "Why not let Ronaldo walk?"

Well, his fingers were stuck firm up a nostril.

And mirror whacked him good on the crown.

McSweeny stood for a second with a happy look as he had gone to a Far Away Land full of mounted police officers in bikinis, you mean female officers, no, either if they wore bikinis.

"Oh, dear what has mirror done?" Beag acting innocent.

"My little alien, come help me, I was only driving you away to save you from him," Ronaldo crawling up the hill.

It was the rattle that made Ronaldo stand up so was a good target for a descending mirror that took him out.

"Let us go Beag," Wayne and mounted a grizzly bear.

Beag got on the mountain lion.

"Miror will bring Dorothy to us and LEG and help us find the Leader of Earth," Beag.

"Yes, and to populate earth with our hybrids," Wayne who was lecherous and more human than Beag so looked forward to meeting Dorothy. A woman he had never met before, why she might have missing teeth, forgotten to remove her curlers, still in her pink fluffy slippers, in an open smokers robe, rolls of tummy hanging over bloomers and her size 49D bra stained with coffee and cigar ash and the goods in the 49D bra over used by suckling kids so hung down to a navel.

Wayne had spent time on a flying saucer.

Wayne could do with a good talking to, maybe his shorts pulled down and a spanking.

Wayne was a Son of Adam.

And Beag and Wayne fed their wild mounts jerky.

The critters were smart, they knew if they ate these two riders that did be end of jerky treats.

Ice Cream Soda Flavoured, always a hit.

Saucer Command 2

The General, aspired to be an emperor.

"If I had been Beag I did be leader of Earth now, Dorothy my queen and my legions ready to conquer Mars, Venus and Pluto," the commander of the flying saucer to his junior officers and although he did not need a mouth to say this, a mouth appeared because he wanted to spray spit over his junior officers to humiliate them.

He was a space traveller and watched many alien movies, especially those from earth.

Most of his junior officers looked green with big black eyes, others were science fiction and yes, it was SPOCK.

Each had thoughts on the subject, some would send what was said to their emperor, others thought of supporting him and getting rich, being governor of Earth, and some said nothing, but all were expendable, even those that said nothing as the emperor would expect them to depose their commander on treason and then the emperor did send them to an arena as they might depose him next.

They were aliens, what do you expect, human decency?

Well, the commander wore a gold necklace with a medallion at the end with his FACE on it.

Not his leader Back on Planet Ajax, that medallion was in a drawer in his sleeping quarters under soiled tissue hankies, hey wait a moment, where is the nose bit on their face, well, it comes out of that black hole for a sneeze and sniff.

Convenient.

A medallion hiding under postcards of Earth girls.

Pictures of Dorothy.

He must be a Peeping Tom?

Even the Sons of Adam were aliens, God gets about.

Well, had this commander manoeuvred his ship so that Beag met her. And from lace curtains across a porthole, he glanced at Dorothy.

The trouble men go to meet a girl.

See, he was a pervert, bet those frillies in the draw are stolen from Dorothy's washing line.

By Gawd, the alien was human, he was obsessed.

You see, in 'Lion King,' is it Simba who looks at the stars and his ancestor reply to him, well, beware it is not ancestors but aliens up there using us as SIMS in a betting game they play called 'Earth.'

Was that a crop duster just fly by Beag and the pilot waved

to him, why because it was an alien pilot and he was heading into the wind to release his dust of weed killer, no, a dust cloud of D.N.A. to alter the human make up to reverse what these aliens been doing, crop dusting for millions of years, turning us from monkeys into humans, and now an alien playing the game 'Earth' just lost a round, so the D.N.A. to be released to make us monkeys again.

"Oik," we will say in the back seats of a cinema watching 'The Day of the Triffids.'

Laying bets on which human leader did use nuclear weapons and win the game, also making sure earth was depopulated of humans for an easy alien conquest.

How do I know all this rubbish, I was abducted by aliens and eves dropped on their conversations, and I read science fiction, I never fib.

And the trouble was?

Have you guessed?

Was it Beag who came last in class.

But not to worry the alien was a trainee pilot and he released his dust early, and the cloud blew back onto the flying saucer.

There was a lot of coughing and sudden urges to eat peanuts, hold tea parties, and do naughty stuff randy monkeys do.

And the general looked for Beag, it was his fault and stuffed the tail growing out of his shorts back into the shorts. It was the emperor's idea go use monkey D.N.A. and the general did empty a vial into a birthday cake for his emperor, as soon as a tail grew the people did put him in a zoo, the emperor must a pure alien, The rouble was the general was one of these folks that never thought ahead, meaning the girl hidden in the cake would have got hungry and had a nibble and grown a nail by the she jumped out wobbling plenty as these aliens kept that stuff in pockets in their bodies, so were not sexless.

They were human after all.

HYBRID, COMEDY SCIENCE FICTION

And the game did be up for the general, his emperor as punishment did make him drink a vial, "Oki."

*

"Ship hover above Beag," and nothing happened as these aliens were used to thought control and this commander of the alien Star Trek Fleet was speaking English for our benefit.

And did the crew obey, of course not, they were looking for peanuts.

So was the fault of the alien crop duster without a flying licence now heading into the Pacific Ocean as forgotten how to turn his plane about.

"It twigged and the flying saucer lurched away at 5,000 m.p.h. and the general was standing gawking ogling an image of

Dorothy driving an R.V. towards Beag along a country trek used by joggers, mountain bikes and hungry mountain lions. Lions who seeing the ship waved their paws at the monkeys at the portholes, honest.

Now we all seen an episode of Star Trek and Willian S. is always sitting in his command swivel chair when ordering, "Warp Speed, oh did we forget to beam Scotty up?" Because he knew if the ship accelerated and you were standing you went 'splat' against the huge command screen where stars, planets and comets were seen and Dorothy.

"SPLAT," yes the sound of the commander hitting a smaller version of the 'Enterprise command screen as this was a low built flying saucer meant to zoom down 'Broadway Street,' in New York before turning left and zig zagging other streets to go demolish New York Zoo, by accident as the alien Coxswain at the joy stick of the saucer controlled by thought was waiting for his commander to peel off the screen, slide to the command floor and self inflate without moaning as he was a looked up to person, their commander to give orders.

And this explains why certain penguins escaped and took over a cargo ship off Madagascar and built an aeroplane for a talking dancing lion, a hypochondriac giraffe, a hippo needing an emergency diet and an egotistic lemur.

Yes, the truth is out at last, and because the government denies the existence of flying saucers, influenced a film company to influence you, a flying saucer was not responsible for escaping these animals, it was penguins.

Please believe this conspiracy theory, penguins are smart, dangerous just waiting to take over the Earth.

And explains why Beag was helped from the crowd of Napoleonic soldiers in front of him by cheer leaders dressed as penguins to keep the moral of the extras up.

"Boom," went the twelve pounders to the music of Beethoven's 1812 Overture.

"What is that chef and drag queen doing in the battle scene, CUT," a director as Beag was still in what Dorothy dressed him in, and Wayne was a top-class chef, so wore his checkered trousers so the world would recognise that and for effect splattered red ketchup on his legs.

"Look Wayne they are coming to welcome us," Beag waving at thundering Cuirassier coming their way.

"Beag," Wayne pulling Beag to back track the way they came.

"Roar," several mountain lions accompanying them in defiance of the French.

"Boom," went the twelve pounders.

"Oh goody, fireworks, they are celebrating our arrival, Dorothy must have told them we are here," Beag unaware the air waves were full of news about him and dangerous drivers on Intestate 5.

Just shows you how innocent Beag was and stupid.

"Oh, director Alba, those are the aliens everyone is looking for," and was whispered by an aide not wanting to alarm the thousands of extras on the film set.

And what is whispered is soon known by all for eves dropping is a common hobby.

"There is a million-dollar reward for the capture of the aliens," and it was an extra and a lot of PLUM. A dead alien did be better than they had an excuse to dissect in Area 51.

And Beag levitated Wayne and all the cute animals following them, so the heavy cavalry charged underneath and went down the bush, through a crash barrier and to the beach.

"Business is brisk today," the hot dog vendor on the beach.

"Jesus," his customers scattering from the charge.

"My hot dog van," the vendor under a cloud of splinters.

And a cannon ball hit Beag in the stomach.

Stars, planets, and Milky Ways shot out of his mouth followed by white doves and butterflies from his bum; Beag was a class of his own, "Owe."

And because Beag was suffering extreme indigestion, stopped levitating, and those running about below ran faster as mountain lions, bears, beavers, and skunks had fallen amongst them.

"Jesus, I swear if you send lightning bolts into these lions to save me, I will become a Wednesday Night church goer," and no lightning bolts came.

"Jesus, save me, stuff these animals with cotton balls and straw, and I will become a nun," from the hot dog vendor and that did not happen.

And the wild things got full eating spilled hot dogs so did not eat anyone, so now Jesus is going to collect on those promises or else.

*

Now back on the saucer the commander needed a dump and as Jesus said, "What goes in goes out," so even if the aliens thought of dumping, they still needed a place to dump as dumping was a personal thing.

"Argh," The Commander sighing reading an alien XXX magazine then added "ARGH," as some aspirer had opened a jar of Planet Cadbury scorpions out in the ventilation shaft above his head.

"Singing in The rain," the commander screamed in tune and jumped here and there in rhythm to avoid the assassins bugs.

Then he opened the door and a lone green Martian dressed as a Roman as been watching earth cartoons stood there with a laser pointed at where his jewels were inside his body. See, told you they had pockets in the skin for a nose, ears, mouth, lips, melons, and jewels.

"I hate you, goodbye bully, slob, greedy, fink, dummy, distant uncle," and should have fired long ago for 1] Those scorpions fed up with being stood upon by the big overweight commander rushed him as an easier standing target.

2] The commander was still quick on the draw and used his laser from a holster that merged with his green body, see the holster was green see.

End of aspirer.

"I must clean up and then get back to my command post and use internal security to hunt down cousins, eh, I mean aspirers," and went his way and the ventilation came on sucking

all the bad essences out of the toilet, and an aspirer in the ventilation shaft with a canvas bag containing a Planet Neptune Puff Adder was never seen again.

Why, the shaft had intelligence and spat out foreign objects into space.

It was just a distant cousin.

And the snake, the intelligent ventilation shaft sucked it back to the ship's zoo where alien zoo attendants caught it, put it in a glass heated tank and fed it MICE.

Later in his command chair the general did notice the aspirer float by.

"That is sergeant Idi, twentieth cousin removed, well I never."

Was anyone loyal to the commander, of course there was, Beag who was void of corrupt thoughts of aspiring to be commander, and then who knows, emperor as Beag was a good alien who only thought of humping LEG and populating earth with his hybrids.

Yes, an alien needing a visit to the vet.

"Pay rise for those who inform on aspirers," the general, "and the anti monkey venom D.N.A. to rid us of tails, peanut butter urges and stop you swinging from the lights is available, at a cost," for the general knew the perks of the trade.

Why aliens were just like humans after all.

CHAPTER 6 DOROTHY ARRIVES

Dorothy allows her red hair loose

"Christ my head," the owner of the R.V. holding onto doorknobs inside his R.V. as Dorothy drove along a hillside road towards Beag.

Road Runners paced the R.V. dodging spinning hub caps.

"I am coming my love," Dorothy, hey, this smooching stuff was a bit quick, perhaps we heard wrong, "I am coming my alien," yes that is what she called.

And how did she know where to go, well she was a savvy woman and had switched on Google's Location Finder on a spare small supermarket mobile and slipped it in a pocket of the body warmer Beag now wore.

"Lady," the owner of the R.V. making it just behind Dorothy at the wheel.

In a hand a toilet roll to beat the daylights out of Dorothy as she drove.

A loo roll, well it was the last place he visited and the only thing handy.

BUT.
Dorothy saw:
1] Beag ahead.
2] Zoo animals.
3] A battle scene with canons.
4] Many campers and cameras.
5] Beag hit with a cannonball.
6] She was sure she heard moans and groans from under the R.V.
7] The end of the loo paper should have been flushed

"He better not be dead after all the trouble I have been through?" Does she say that or?

"PLUM, the poor thing must be dead, poor little alien," or did she say? "I can still sell the alien dead body to cover my legal expenses," or, "I can stuff the dead cute alien to be a soft toy for the pets," was it, "Hey mister, drop the toilet roll before I slam

the brakes and then beat the day lights out of you, understand?" And Dorothy saw the end of the loo paper and knew she was going to beat the daylights out of this man.
AND.
"I can always make a spoof of 'Napoleon' and even if rubbish with my name will be a best seller at the movies. The Film Director watching the R.V. mow through a line of red coat English Line Infantry.

"She is beautiful, she can be in 'Johnny English 66'," the Film Director seeing Dorothy in the big side mirror.

And Beag held onto his mirror and Wayne him as he like Thor flew towards Dorothy and LEG. Had he not put Dorothy and LEG together yet?

Leg did stick out of Dorothy's body where her moons were.
He was not human.

He was not familiar with human anatomy apart from classes he came last in.

He was an alien.

One full of alien testerone.

Therefore, it must be asked, "Where did aliens get the intelligence to Star travel?"

And Beag came close to the Film Director who gaped, "E.T." and as Beag's mirror flew over his head, Jetstream dislodged the director's wig.

"Owe," the cast about him.

"Look shaving cuts on his head," one of the cast.

"Yes, band aid also," a cook.

"Must wear a wig as has lice, I read about that in a history lesson of colonial America," a dish washer.

Then Dorothy ran over him and lucky for him the R.V. had a high chassis or he did be in emergency and why he was not, "Where is he?" The film crew asked as the R.V. drove away over emerging baby cacti, thorny sage bush, basking rattlers, and the thousands crew extras lined up as there was only one mobile latrine to save on costs.

"I had expensive yoga lessons from an Indian Guru friend of The Beatles who taught me to block out pain, and my Kung Fu Teachers taught me how-to pick-up balling balls with my teeth, so am lucky there as am holding onto the engine cover of this R.V. with them as I want that alien and I will be on 'Time,' and who knows, invited back to the alien planet to make a movie about them, then be The President of The U.S.A.

I will replace 'Coco Pops' as a household name," the Film Director who did need emergency after all and like 'Nosferatu,' the vampire made his way to the driver window using the suction of his palms and wet tongue and breathing his tummy in out as taught by his Guru?

It was disgusting and he had an idea, "I will remake The Fly."

Suspense.

AT SAME TIME.

And Beag blew in a side window of the R.V.

HYBRID, COMEDY SCIENCE FICTION

"Saved," were his words just as the owner of the R.V. free from toilet roll snatched him and stuffed Beag into an overnight bag.

"Where is my friend?" Wayne asked.

Greed shook the owner of the R.V. as he realised there were two aliens, and this one was human looking.

Wayne with regrets he had to leave as there was nothing to stuff him into. His wig, wigs get about, his vest, his silk 'Y' Fronts, his extra-large size socks that doubled at Christmas to hang above a fire and burn so he never got presents so hated Santa. And what did he want from Santa, he had no idea so got nothing.

AT THE SAME TIME.

And now this Nosferatu crawled to the R.V. roof, where thinking there was no need to suck in his belly and used his palms to hang on as he tied up his appearance, so the wind blew him away.

"Lucky my Guru taught me pain is all in the head as I grasp the rear emergency exit stairs and pull myself up them to the R.V. roof and sit there using the muscles on my moons to grasp the R.V. roof as taught me by my Guru.

Where the wind blew his eyes to the back of his head, and perhaps explains why he had no idea what to do next. Grasshoppers, flying bugs and spiders on silk threads had gotten into his eyes.

What would you do reader?

1] Try and wipe your eyes clean.

2] Relax your moon muscles as bus crawl everywhere so has bugs in his pants.

3] So is blown put of this tale.

4] And sue the Guru for he experienced PAIN.

Then the R.V. stopped.

He could see nothing, flying grit had filled his eyes,

pollinating plant seeds also.
>Sea gull mess.
>Condor mess.
>A BB pellet?

AT THE SAME TIME
>The owner of the R.V. tittered behind Dorothy holding the loo paper roll.
>But a great fear of that woman did posses him, that woman who had locked him in the R.V. latrine, a woman who had warned him about using second hand loo paper to threaten her with.
>The pitiful thing was terrified.
>Then he had an idea, he would bargain with the crazy woman at the R.V. wheel for a share of rewards for capturing an alien or he did throw the overnight bag out of the R.V.
>Yes, that was what he did do, it was a brilliant idea.
>Let us laugh insanely.
>He was asking for Dorothy to beat the day lights out of him.
>What would you think of in this situation reader?
>Oh, still holding the threatening loo roll?

The R.V. had stopped, a camper stopped along side it, the cast of Shrek came aboard the R.V.
Where did stooges come from, they are in camper

>And the back of his head was slapped, a finger relaxed on the bag, The Stooges noticed. Nine more slaps came and that made nine relaxed fingers.
>"Mo, slap him harder and ask him where the alien is, better still, where Dorothy is, we did steal her camper Mo," Larry urged and was slapped over the use of some of his words.
>Hope filled the owner of the R.V., they had no idea where the alien was and there was a camper nearby, he could make his getaway in, he still held the bad with one finger circling about

the top.

Trouble was he was doomed.

"Hello, we girls should stick together?" Susanna Lou below as Dorothy got out. The girl showed no fear, life had been tough, she wanted a share of the alien reward and stood like Napoleon.

For an answer Freckles and Jack jumped her. Maybe if she had a threatening toilet roll it might have been different?

Dorothy strode over them and attracted by slapping made her way to the roof of the R.V. as she knew The Stooges were not up there. She needed a break, she needed to think, an awkward thing to do with the slapping and pet shredding sounds.

Someone was on the roof.

AT THE SAME TIME

There was a screech of brakes as a delivery van skidded to a halt sideways as they do in films showering all in dry bush and

rattlers so Susanna shaking the serpents and pets off got in the R.V. and shut and locked the doors in the driver's cab.

Gave a middle finger, stuck out a tongue in a grotesque fashion and wiggled her ears with the help of hands.

"Her name was Susanna,

Not of Holly Wood fame

Just the girl next door," and it was The Stooges doing the musical part dancing too, waving at you for they were 'Funny Men.'

AND.

The owner of the R.V. appeared at the back exit window covered in Freckles and jack. Those ferocious pets got about, I mean one minute they was licking and cuddling Susanna and because they got bored sought new friends.

The face of the Stooges competed with them there making faces gesticulating, screaming even, what message were they trying to get across, oh, "Save us."

From whom?

From the pets?

The R.V. owner?

The driver at the wheel?

Yes, the girl from next door was at the wheel with no licence.

It was time for Wayne to make a name for himself in this tale as a hero. One minute Susanna Lou was sitting in the driver's seat looking at all the dials and levers remembering

her console racing games and her cycling, there was no difference, you just turned the key that was begging her to and off you go.

See the girl from next door was about to drive without a licence.

That is when Wayne being small crawled along the floor and emerged between her legs.

Susanna stared at him horrified.

"What the hell are you?" She asked remembering a film, 'The Zombie Undead.'

Then Wayne remembered Beag's mission to Planet Earth and grinned.

That made Susanna scream and turn the ignition key, why, it was the last thingmabob her brain was going to do before Wayne arrived between her knees salivating all over the place holding a knife and fork, remember he was part alien.

All rubbish the knife and fork.

It was hot down there amongst the pedals and toenail varnish, and had started to salivate to lick his lips and places, PLACES?

What would you do if in her place and a head appeared between your legs.

1] Have a cardiac arrest.

2] Smile.

3] "The troll of my dreams."

4] Show 2 fingers to your eyes then poke it in the eyes.

5] She did not know Wayne was from Saucer Command or might settle for him and forget Beag. "And here is the alien, hello, it is a human chef," the news reader and Susanna Lou did be booted off the air waves.
ANYWAY.

Dorothy did a dance and jig throwing the rubber snakes off that wrapped about her feet and not concentrating where she put her feet tumbled down the embankment.

Rubber snakes, of course, real ones bite and because they were rubber Dorothy bounced and was not scratched.

Below folk ran about avoiding the raining rubber snakes.

"PLUM," they cursed catching snakes by the tales and swinging them in the air to let go so they wrapped about someone.

Out came the hidden automatic assault rifle self assembly, but "Hey these snakes are rubber, I knew that I just wanted to know if you knew," and tucked away the rifle in unassembled parts.

It was something out of the Bible when Moses crossed a desert and God gave them serpents to bite the jew sore."

And a film director watched and had an idea for a film, it would be called 'Exodus.'

BLAH, Dorothy and R.V. where heading for a crash barrier, and would there be any hot dogs left if she were hungry?
AND.

"We have stopped, now to get out of this hell," The film director under the R.V. and crawled out chewing a rubber serpent.

That is when the R.V. owner unable to see and fed up being slapped dropped the overnight bag over the R.V. roof.

"THUD," very loudly.

A scream and the rev of an engine.

The side door of the R.V. swung open and a black bag was

thrown in and a messed-up man needing emergency crawled in, the director and he spat the rubber toy out.

"A hobo?" Susanna seeing him and put her foot down on the gas pedal.

Why, no idea, it was handy for her to let off stress.

The stress was let off below too as did foil any would be attacker sneaking up behind her.

It was lethal, what had she been eating, oh yeh, stuff days old in Diego's eatery

She had learned a few minutes earlier that was the pedal to push down to get speed.

The hobo shouted, "He is in the bag, help me," as the hobo who was the film director lost his balance and something was moving in his pants, what?

Was it a hand reaching up behind him?

No, just where had he been lately?

Under the R.V. meeting wildlife.

Oh, dear was it a rubber rattler about to bite important places.

Then a gopher's head appeared and showed what big chiselling teeth it owned.

"Oh, Sweet Jesus no," the film director and did not say please.

And with a gopher nipping his moons fell backwards out of the R.V.

"Help," he shouted but no one did, he was a hobo.

"Quick a soft landing," Mo using his walnut and jumped from the R.V.

Curly Jo hesitated so Larry pushed him out and jumped having all those under him making his soft landing.

They were back in the camper.

Guess who was driving?

"Where are the brakes?" Larry screamed and Mo dropped his mouth, Curly Joe covered his eyes with his hands, that hobo was standing in the road it seemed looking for something in his 'Y' Fronts, and once again the film director found himself under a vehicle minus the cute gopher that had the intelligence to leap from him at the last moment before collision.

Mo opened his eyes, there was no sign of the man and sighing momentarily went back to slapping Larry to go faster.

Curly Joe tried to concentrate on strange sounds coming from under the camper. "Bump bumpety bump, groan moan help," the strange sounds.

He was not sure he heard, "Help me you fools," and calling prospective helpers fools would not get you any help, so Curly Joe shrugged and slapped Mo as he always did, and soon there was mayhem, so who was steering?

You, not me.

And Dorothy screamed, why, her camper was heading for her, would you not scream, no, of course not, you did puff and huff and hold up a badge out of Corn Flakes, 'L.A. Police,' instead and visit emergency.

Dorothy was a girl, girls scream.

Who would save Dorothy?

Super woman, no, she did show Dorothy up by not screaming and holding a handout to stop the camper.
AND.
"I hear a high pitch wail that hurts my ears, I must put a stop to it," the delivery driver and wrecked his companies van as it was not an off-road vehicle. It did have a foghorn the driver was supposed to use on delivery notifying the recipient a parcel was here and the sound so loud birds flew, gophers borrowed, coyotes howled, vultures dropped from the sky and the recipient clutched a chest and fell flat.

"I will toss the parcel towards the porch, take a photo of proof of delivery and be off to finish my twelve-hour shift," the delivery driver said seeing the source of the melodious wail, Dorothy,
SPOKE.

"It is her, I will run her over a few times and throw her in the back with the other parcels and head somewhere quiet, like the beach and there question her as to where the alien is? She better tell me as I need the reward money as I will be sacked, then I can start a new life in Canada as a prawn farmer in a disused swimming pool as a tank," the driver and let us look at his

driving licence on the dashboard, well I never, it is a Philippine Licence, and the name is Phillipo.

Are you wondering is it another cousin of those other two, **READ ON.**

"Holy Moses, that camper is going to run down that wonder woman from the eatery, and that delivery van I recognise from the F.B.I. Most wanted list as a "The Delivery Van Robber," with a $10,000 reward for capture **DEAD**, just where is my pistol and I need a boulder to stand on to get a good shot at the fugitive."

That is when the mobsters fired at him as mobsters shoot first then ask questions.

Bullets zinged past Mcsweeny, "ZING," see what I mean.

And the mobsters were all puffed, sweaty and dirty, covered in flies as flies like sweaty dirty folk and the mobsters were in that condition as they had pushed the limousine with the godfather in through the crash barrier to the beach below where watchers took mobiles of them.'

Soon their faces did be over news channels and the god father's family want to give them that kiss on the cheeks we all know what that means as watched the film, 'Godfather.'

Who did save McSweeney.

You, ha Ho he, make me laugh.

It was a fire engine with a desperate man at the wheel that saved McSweeny.

How?

Diego had no H.G.V. licence so was a bad as Larry at the wheel of the camper or the girl next door in the R.V.

But he was enjoying himself, ever since childhood he had wanted to drive a fire truck but as a child, he could not reach the pedals and the wheel at the same time.

He could now and the foghorn.

"Holy Mother of Jesus what is that?" One of the mobsters a good R.C.

"The godfather return," a second mobster.

"Give it to him," a third and took from a violin case a Thomson Machine gun and fired at the fire truck.

"Sure, I heard the godfather shout PLUM," the fourth mobster trying to figure out what the godfather had shouted.

In fact, Diego had shouted, "PLUMS who are those idiots firing guns at me," and hid under the wheel so the truck picked up speed, why, because Diego is a big muscular man and his moons where on the gas pedal and he was swearing, "I am stuck down here, it is also hot, and my crotch is sweaty and itchy."

"Run," mobster number one and mobster number two from a pocket took a cheese wire and did a nasty with these words, "Godfather I slay your assassin," for he was a cringing save my own neck type and hoped the crime family did not kiss his cheeks.

And mobster number three thought about this action and liked it so from a shoulder holster took a four-foot-long machete and used it.

"That leaves only me," number four mobster wiping his flick blade machete off on number three.

Then the fire truck ran over him so there were no mobsters left to shoot McSweeny.

And the fire truck ladder swung away and hit McSweeny on the head, so his shoulder was between the railings and with a dazed look he held onto the ladder that swung out and his feet wrapped about Dorothy, and he wrapped his oily legs about her lifting her up and away.

Oily legs as that is what Dorothy saw them as, *a man was trying it on.*

He was, McSweeny thought Dorothy was Wonder Woman, the fink.

And the camper smashed into the fire truck that was so big and heavy suffered minor damage.

But what about The Stooges in the camper, were they scattered about the road moaning waiting for emergency?

Who knows how a Stooge thinks?

AND.

And the R.V. with Wayne between Susanna Lou's legs hit the back of the camper.

"WHAM BANG."

Wayne's head hit elastic with the collision and Susanna a woman of the world had plenty of experience with his type, so used his head as a drum, his lugs as exercise stretchers, his eyes as dart boards for her painted fingernails, his tongue as a roll of measuring tape, his lips as things to pull, punch and rip off.

"God of chefs save me," Wayne but the collision had wedged him good.

Who would save Wayne.

Did he want saved from where he was?

Freckles and Jack were now sitting next to Susanna, the cab door having bounced open.

Susanna stopped what she was doing to Wayne, it was the innocent looking stare from the animals that told her to search her frills for cat and dog treats.

No luck so a lot of s creaming came from that drivers cab as the animals knew Susanna was too angelic and beautiful looking to deserve what was coming.

"Oh God of Chefs, you do not hear me, help," Wayne.

Yeh Wayne got mauled.

And who saved him.

IT HAPPENED SO.

WELL, The R.V. door opened, and someone crawled in, it

was a famous film director covered in muck. He not only looked like a zombie but sounded like one and he approached the cab.

The animals took fright and lept out the R.V. window into the camper where the stooges were.

ALIVE, they were The Three Stooges.

Oh dear, just what was Dorothy teaching and feeding these animals?

And Ronaldo collapsed under Dorothy clinging to McSweeny on the fire ladder and reached up and took hold of her legs.

"Where is the little PLUM?" He asked her accidently pulling down her trousers, and you must ask, did she shave her legs, yes, she did. Her legs where so smooth Ronaldo was having problems holding onto them.

"PLUM<" he swore often.

Think Dorothy would be angry about that and what advice could you give Ronaldo?

1 Run.

2 Beg forgiveness.

3 Blame the others.

4 Promise her, her own aeroplane.

5 Just when you are free, please do not beat the day lights out of me as I am desperate
    fugitive and dangerous.

6 Keep ogling.

So, they were all together but was Beag?

In a black bag the owner of the R.V. was seen sneaking away with. If he had not been sneaking no suspicion did have been aroused.

It was the tip toeing that did it.

He stood on a twig that broke making a "SNAP," sound.

"PLUM is this a rubber rattler I just stood on," he hopes so they heard him sneaking.

"Beag," Dorothy shouted fed up with her position.

"LEG," came from the black bag and it levitated.

"Oh Christ," the R.V. owner sixty feet above ground as Beag levitated towards LEG.

And a collection of animals hearing Beag came out of nowhere.

"Are they going to eat us?" Susanna asked.

Those gophers had big teeth.

"Curly stand in front of me," and as Curly hesitated Mo slapped.

Then mirror appeared and with laser light cut open the black bag, so Beag levitated out.

"Beautiful an angel," Susanna showing she had hope.

"A leprechaun," Mo showing what he thought of most, The Luck of The Irish.

"Rumpelstiltskin with a favour," Curly wanting a better life than slapping.

"Puss and Boots," Curly Joe showing his mental age and was slapped by two.

"If I had that ability, I did be Robo Cop and rich," McSweeny.

"But you do not," Dorothy raking his legs as she knew he was trying it on with his legs about her.

Did she not realise that those legs were saving her a drop?

They belonged to McSweeny, that was what mattered.

"I must have that alien to chauffeur me to Oscar Awards with levitation," the film director trying to dislodge a protected salamander from an ear, and what else had he picked up under the vehicles, that extra bulge but this is a clean tale so must be a rabid racoon, yes that it what it is.

And Beag floated in the sky, his arms held out promising salvation.

"It is the Holy Mother," the delivery driver because he had been a good church goer.

"It is a blow-up advertisement for hot dogs," Diego distracted by ogling.

"No stupid, it is my alien," Ronaldo getting it right.

AND we all know it is Beag levitating.

And as the bag was empty there was no one levitating the R.V. owner who fell and rolled down the bush, through a crash barrier and to a waiting crowd below.

Some in that crowd held open hand cuffs ready to use.

Would the R.V. owner be saved and not meet these law enforcement officers.

Would he like you and me claim reward for information leading to the capture of aliens and dangerous fugitives?

It was worth a try.

"Look there is the alien," he shouted and as the beach watchers said, "Owe," scampered back up the cliff he had come down.

That was smart.

And no one saved Wayne whose small head was now at Susanna's knees so was not looking at Beag levitating as was busy.

He had this horrid grin.

Susanna was petrified.

From her elastic she took a pepper spray all girls next door have and sprayed.

Wayne was no longer grinning.

And that explains why Susanna looking down went mental and Wayne lied saying, "Please do not best the PLUMS out of me as I am an alien also with a mission."

Yes, a typical manly explanation towards trying it on.

"Pervert," Susanna as she legged Wayne through the air.

He was small enough to do so.
Where did he land?
The few hundred feet below to the beach?
On the angry gophers with big chiselling teeth?
On rubber rattlers?
On a spot marked, "GO TO JAIL?"

No, the God of Chefs was awake, and Wayne landed in the arms of Beag that immediately brought out suspicious "OWE," from the watchers.

They had dirty minds this lot.

CHAPTER 7 A COUNCIL

The long table

Now all the chasers took positions from an American Football game to charge Beag and stuff him in a black bag, must be the R.V. owner, stuff down a large pair of trousers, perhaps Mo's as his were baggy and needing pressed and what would Beag encounter there?

Stuff down the R.V. loo, perhaps a film director wanting to dish out what it is like living under a vehicle chasses blaming

life on Beag, making sure he was jammed in for no one messes with a film director, no not that, down elastics, if LEGS were attached and whose elastics?

Stuff Susanna, no she tightened her belt as Wayne had taught her what aliens were all ABOUT, stuff Dorothy, well she needed trousers put on and something ought to be done with Wayne who was volunteering to take Beag's place, or stuff down inside a pair of smelly size 11 shoes so must be McSweeny, And the delivery van driver approached with ducting tape for a delivery van driver without tape is not well places upstairs and where would he stuff Beag and had no idea so see, so was thick as toast.

And Diego was thinking of stuffing Beag between hot dog rolls as that is how a food seller vendor thinks, but not Ronaldo who was thinking of making a run for Beag and keep running with the alien in his hands from the others, laughing greedily all the way through crash barriers to watchers below so was not stuffing.

"LEG Take me to your leader," and was Beag who broke the tension.

And Wayne jumped off Beag and marched to Dorothy, "LEG," he moaned and started to smooch a leg.

By habit Wayne pored ketchup on that leg as all good chefs carry ketchup and think of food.

Dorothy looked down at him, see saw a human coming it on.

There was a woosh of martial art legs and Wayne disappeared, out of this story, yes or no, you vote.

"We need to get our act together or we will get nowhere," Susanna wisely.

The slapping going on with The Stooges stopped.

"You mean be friends?" Diego thinking murderous thoughts.

"Yes, we form a convoy and drive together with the alien in the middle vehicle, that way those upfront can watch that vehicle in the mirror and those behind can watch, all making sure Beag is where he should be, in the middle" Susanna explaining wisely and whoever listened to wisdom.

"As long as he is with me in the middle vehicle that is fine by me," Dorothy, well it was her alien.

"Why you, I am a better driver than you," Ronaldo wanting to drive with Beag where he could think up devious plans to get away from the others like putting his foot in the gas and speeding away, well, he had not learned anything, and was it because of the way Diego treated him, as a LOSER always borrowing stuff and never repaying, or was it because he was RONALDO?

Yes, it was because he was Ronaldo, see there is little room for 'Court Ordered Social Work Reports,' here was a fink, plain and simple.

There was the sound of a karate chop descending and Ronaldo lay at Dorothy's feet where aliens from Warner Brother cartoons span about his head.

How many vehicles do we have?" The delivery driver

Phillipo thinking his should be in the middle of the convoy so if the convoy had to break up for a reason, he did speed away with Beag.

"A fire truck," Diego and pulled the foghorn proudly but was descended upon by stooges warning him to be quiet.

And they left him reeling black and blue for The Stooges have perfected the art of slapping into a deadly weapon. "Ha So Chop."

It was hard to notice as Diego still glowed from his other sores.

Some never learn.

"Give me paracetamol," he moaned.

"We have the R.V. with a working television for the aliens to watch," the R.V. owner thinking since they were in his vehicle, he could claim ownership of the aliens.

"Our camper has a television and radio," The Stooges.

"Your camper?" Dorothy and shook each Stooge so three heads rattled as had walnuts in there and not brains.

And Freckles and Jack seeing Dorothy needed help helped.

And none of the others tried to stop the mauling done.

"Bravo Stooges, what an animal act," a chorus from admiring onlookers.

"Yes, Warner Brothers will hire the animals," also.

"What about them?"

"Who?"

"You mean The Stooges?"

"Yes."

"Never heard of them," for the watchers were humans except Diego who held out a wavering hand.

"Owe," came from all as light came forth and dog and cat treats flowed from that hand to the animals. It was an illusion of light; a trick Diego had learned in the Philippines to distract customers as he fleeced their pockets as an intern dish washer.

But he was not an alien and Beag did not like the grease stuck about his mouth so with a click of his thumb all the valuables he just stole dropped to his feet.

"Titter, I have no idea how they got there," and promised when he had Beag he did turn him into a Juke Box in his new eatery the reward money did buy him, hey wait a mo., did he not realise if he got the reward money, he did not have Beag, another thick as toast cousin.

Then those he fleeced beat the daylights out of him, even the pets joined in because they were mean pets.

So

"Well, I will decide for all as I am the law here," McSweeny picking Beag up and he still wore his size 11 shoes, and "Dorothy we take the R.V. in the middle of the convoy.

"Who made you leader?" Phillipo and McSweeny stuck his magnum from a shoulder holster up Phillipo's nose so gooey bits hung from the barrel.

You could see Mcsweeny was not happy and Phillipo not popular with him.

And McSweeney used Phillipo's coloured shirt to wipe clean his pistol.

Philippo did not mind, see with these words, "Let me lick your gun barrel clean officer?" For Phillipo was a grovelling undocumented immigrant who wanted LIFE.

And McSweeny put his pistol away with a look that said it all, "Touch my gun and get digging your grave mister delivery driver."

Dorothy shook her head, who was she to judge a man,

HYBRID, COMEDY SCIENCE FICTION

why she was still minus trousers thanks to that other illegal, immigrant.

"What, Dorothy has no trousers on?" Only the male passengers coming to realise this as were Sons Of Adam.

So, it was decided McSweeny and Dorothy would take the

middle vehicle and Beag.

Who decided, a magnum did.

And Dorothy waved her C.I.A. badge in the air as to say, if he is a lawman then I am Captain Kirk of the Star Ship Enterprise.

Is McSweeny a real policeman?
Is Dorothy's C.I.A. badge from the bottom of a 'Corn Flake,' box?
And Susanna went up front with The Stooges as she did not want to be alone with the cousins for their eyes followed her, so goosebumps flourished on her neck.
A wise move, The Stooges never thought of women, only jobs, wages, and unemployment.
And Diego got in the fire truck and shut the door in the face of Ronaldo once again.
Who would offer Ronaldo wandering about holding his nose a seat in a vehicle or just leave him.
"Hey cousin, I have room in my delivery van," and yes Phillipo is related to Ronaldo and Diego, so world watch out.

And the engines did rev, and exhaust choked as windows where open and we must ask two questions?
What about Wayne?
Look, what is that running seen in the rear mirrors, it is Wayne.
Why is he running?
He is afraid of being left lonesome without means of

90

support.

What are those animals behind doing?

The mountain lions and bears and skunks all attracted to the light shining from Beag wanting Beag to sit at his alien feet admiringly looking at him with loving eyes.

To eat Beag as all got hungry desires?

To keep him away from humans?

To demand a share of the alien reward?

Who knows you need to be an animal to answer that?

These animals are running behind Wayne.

Wayne you better run fast.

And he did, up the back of a fire truck, onto the roof of a delivery van making dents on the roof, and onto the roof of the R.V. and jumped to the camper thinking Beag did be leading.

The fool, he was wrong, Susanna was here and knew how to deal with him.

The Stooges pulled him in and as Susanna was driving, Wayne was spared her lesson in how to deal with him, but not all The Stooges, "He is one of the aliens," Larry thinking riches and no more soup kitchens.

"Yeh, but we are sharing with the others as one for one and one for all," and Mo slapped him good.

"Yeh," do you think the others saw him come this way Mo?" Yes, they were The Three Stooges and they looked at the back of Susanna's head, she EITHER joined them or OUT and Larry could drive again.

Yes, the convoy had not gone far across country farm roads as listening to the broadcasts knew the police were after them.

And what about McSweeny?

He was a deserter as a real policeman would arrest the lot and hand over Beag and watch his Boss promoted on Fox News as he ate greasy burgers from a roadside eatery, Diego's.

He was thinking self, he was thinking of him and Dorothy on a Caribbean cruise with new identities and his boss eating in a greasy eatery, Diego's.

Had he asked her, nope, why, because he was a Son of Adam.

He had asked his holster pistol though.

What was her reply?

There was a click as the safety went off and McSweeny heard, "Look at that cheap hussy and I will blow your toes off, maybe some place else."

The pistol was a girl.

A jealous female.

A loaded 9 mm with nine shots leaving one toe, how kind.

And wanting you to believe he carries a talking gun with him?

Why not?

Shrek had a talking donkey.

Or either Mcsweeny was hearing voices in his head and needed serious help.

Beware Dorothy you are his little 'Red Riding Hood,' and stay away from him.

And this advice was free.

And the convoy moved and soon a madman emerged amongst them, a man living in oil and grime, he was the film director and had crawled up the toilet bowel from his place amongst the chassis of the R.V.

Therefore, he stunk a bit.

His aim was to overpower the driver with fright as he knew he looked a 'CLOWN,' dripping oil and hoped to snatch Beag and be off.

Off where?

Way back to his film crew two miles behind where he had a million extras dressed as Napoleonic soldiers, but would they recognise him, no, just as an extra from the 'Monster from The Oily Lagoon,' come to steal their acting places so they did beat the blazes out of their boss.

A million beatings would there be anything left of the film director, yes, the 'Monster from The Oily Lagoon,' would be left.

But a mirror belonging to Beag appeared in front of him and he saw himself and screaming in fright collapsed knocking his head against a toilet brush and was unconscious.

The toilet brush Handle was made of rigid plastic.

The convoy stopped.

Dorothy was stuffing this oily man down the loo bowel or trying to. See he was so oily he was difficult to get a grip with, *he was an oily character this film director.*

It was Dorothy's idea to slip him away out the waste pipe and be rid of him.

That is when McSweeny locked her in the loo with the oily man as he saw his chance to drive off with Beag and a jealous gun.

Sort off.

"Want to mud wrestle, do we?" We hear the oily man to Dorothy.

There was squelching slippery sounds.

Was this the end of Dorothy S THE 'Monster from The Oily Lagoon,' OVERPOWERED HER.

Was the oily man a disturbed man who now was on the verge of becoming the nations most wanted oily murderer?

Not so for Dorothy knew her Ha So chop.

Anyway.

Susanna the girl from next door did not check her mirrors while driving so did not realise the R.V. had stopped.

And the delivery van driver with Ronaldo were fighting as Ronaldo the cheap stake was throttling his distant cousin as he did not want to share the alien reward with anyone, so the delivery van drove into the back of the R.V.

SMASH.

This allowed Phillipo a breathing space and to poke Ronaldo

places like the eyes, pull his tongue out three feet, amazing, pull his underwear up over his head and was about to throw him out when the collision happened to their delivery van.

And a fire truck with Diego pretending to be a fireman pulling the foghorn, swivelling the ladder, flicking the blue flashing lights on and off, trying helmets on to fit, was not driving so demolished the delivery van.

Could anyone survive?

Your parcel of plastic flowers to your girl friend was squashed.

The MING vase was now bits.

A rare violin in a case was firewood.

A D.I.Y. Grand Piano now was a D.I.Y. boat.

A collection of rare 'Super MAN' comics now floated across the State.

A flea circus was bust open and where did the fleas go?

Yes, Phillipo would be sacked when his International Driving Licence turned out to be an International Date Club Membership card.

Phillipo better run.

Survive they did, Phillipo crawled of the bust radiator out looking like he just did ten rounds with Mohammed Ali, and then a man with underwear pulled up over his head as he still wore trousers fell out of a hub cap, bet that hurt.

And it was Freckles and Jack that watched all from the back of the camper as it happily drove away.

Why?

Wayne was free and sitting on Susanna's lap helping her steer.

He kept turning his head to ogle her his reward for driving.

He managed this as he was a REAL OILY CHARACTER needing no oil to be oily.

And Susanna went mental, and Wayne began to realise Earth girls did not find him attractive, so he began to sob.

And Susanna stopped beating the PLUM out of him and began to molly cully him.

The foolish girl.

If she were double jointed, she could drop her head or better twist Wayne's head about, she did see he was grinning.

Wayne had his own mission, to steal Beag's mission and that was to populate Planet Earth with hybrids.

And if The Stooges had not sneaked up and slapped the day lights out of him and pushed him out a window his crocodile tears might have in his imagination got him places. And it was The Stooges comforting Sussanne that explains why the camper drove into a roadside tree and hot water burst from the radiator.

Wayne's fault.

"Let us kill the little PLUM" unanimous voices from the camper.

What a collection of friends.

And animals understand English, so Freckles and Jack got acquainted with Wayne.

Do not fret, a good chef always keeps tasty treats in his deep pockets for such occasions, a strip of Jerky for Jack and a fishy biscuits for Freckles.

Not a lie and is the truth.

Why this chef had learned alien ways, he could speak DOOLITTLE.

Did that save him from those upfront?

No, it was his fault the camper was in a tree.

Jack was happy, he had a tree.

Were these folks really hoping to stay together and divide the alien reward?

And Dorothy always remembered, "Take me to your leader LEG."

And Beag had enough of being stuffed places and wanted his LEG so like a dog howled as McSweeny tried to manoeuvre the R.V. out of the wreckage of the convoy.

His ears went POP.

Why he was covering them as Beag was levitating behind his head howling.

Then mirror appeared and a rubber ball shot forth and mirror played pin pong on McSweeny's head.

"PING," the ball went forty times.

"Christ," McSweeny forty times.

Except this alien rubber was designed to attach on contact an alien surface, so lumps of McSween's golden hair went with each "PING."

"Oh, my Gawd," McSweeny leaping from the cab of the R.V. into the waiting arms of the other drivers to catch him, no, they stood back and allowed him to hit dirt.

Would you try to catch a man who weighed what, half a tonne from eating doughnuts at roadside greasy eateries and as desert triple blue cheese steak burgers fried in LARD as Diego was a cheap stake, followed by a jar of sauerkraut, a jar of gherkins, a bottle of watery ketchup and a dozen friend eggs sunny side up?

Could this man gas?

And the squelchy sounds from inside the R.V. attracted Beag, "Dorothy," he said as being an alien unlike the humans beside him could not recognise her brand of squelch.

And the R.V. door flew open just as McSweeney was getting up.

Square on the moons so he catapulted away into the arms of Wayne approaching thinking he was safe from Susanna now Dorothy was back.

Back, where was he?

He was half human remember.

And oil dripped off Dorothy in loud plops.

"LEG," Beag and went to cuddle a leg but failed as it was so OILY.

And the men, even McSweeny recovered to look holding Wayne, for Dorothy wrestling in oil had lost her jacket and shirt.

Lucky she still had her pants on and had not burned her bra as a suffragette.

And Beag listened to his mirror that out of her surface produced degreaser for Dorothy, the oily man could remain oily for he was an oily character.

And Susanna went and opened her suit case and showed Dorothy women clothes, all fit for floozy occasions trying to influence a film director to give her a part as the unnamed milk maid that Dracula bites, a bank manager for an overdraft sitting on his desk and not chair flicking pumpkin seeds at his face to be cheeky showing elastics, so never got the loan as the manager was allergic to pumpkin, a traffic cop to rip up the jay walking ticket by rolling up a skirt to show a knee so got the ticket as the officer was in a happy relationship, and perhaps get Wayne to pester Dorothy and not her.

She was a kind caring girl our Susanna who just needed a break, *will you give her a break? Your credit card and keys to your house and car?*

There was the sound of a shower and a happy girl singing nursery songs, 'Hickory, Dickory, dock,' 'Jack Sprat,' Pat a cake pat a cake baker's man,' then did a solo 'Taylor Swift,' and all were spell bound.

Then she appeared smelling nice, of soap, shampoo and deodorant under a pink Stetson, cow hide body warmer and shorts and blue cowboy boots, yes, do we laugh or ogle?

We ogle.

Who laughed/

"We got to stick together or we loose," she said and looked about for a challenger. There was a slap as Mo silenced Larry.

"I will lead us to riches," Dorothy continued and taking Beag's hands indicated he levitate her to the roof of the R.V.

SILENCE.

There was slapping as Mo slapped Curly Jo.

Later the men did complain of stiff necks ogling up at Dorothy as she pranced on the R.V. roof waving her hands to illustrate riches to be gained.

And Jack pranced besides her and Freckles being a cat sat calmly looking at the folk below as if they were idiotic PLUMS.

HYBRID, COMEDY SCIENCE FICTION

How to escape the law Dorothy could see coming their way from up here.

What would happen to any of them who cheated on the rest.

SILENCE.

There was the sound of two slaps as Mo got what he dished.

Even Susanna was impressed and mentally taking notes on how to improve her routine with landlords, officers, bank managers AND YOU for a loan.

A loan she did not pay back as the only acting parts she got was an unnamed milk maid
being bitten by Dracula.

In future she did wear blue cowboy boots and tap dance on the bank manager's desk scattering loan files and be thrown out by security as the manager had seen it all before.

The police officer did arrest her for solicitating as in that attire did look like a gender-affirming procedure drug addict seeking a client.

And would you give her a treat, a meal in Diego's greasy roadside eatery?

Poor Susanna.

SILENCE.

A lot of slapping as The Stooges wanting the latrine did not want to stop looking at Dorothy. Ask them why the slapping, to forget the need to relieve oneself and because they were The Stooges. Ask them if they understood what Dorothy was saying?

Ask all the men present?

"What was Dorothy saying, sorry was listening to music on my mobile," McSweeny **lying** as was spell bound by what was in the blue cowboy boots.

"I was looking at the weather not her legs," Diego **lying so his nose twitched wanting** to grow.

"Sorry was revising my law degree," Ronaldo with a bigger lie so his ears waved.

"What did I miss?" The film director all clean and smelling nice and threw his oily towel away so it wrapped about a nose that had grown, honest and he was lying as being a film producer was always on the look out for talented LEGS so missed naught for, *he was an oily character.*

"I am hooked," Phillipo not lying as he ogled Dorothy atop the R.V. so lost his balance and fell off.

Someone must be more villainous than the others so even Phillipo seems deserving of your sympathy.

And Dorothy the show girl did somersault and Beag flew up and caught her.

Jack jumped up and hung onto her pants, so moons showed.

Trust the dog.

Freckles being calm just sat there.

SILENCE as if the men had never seen moons before. Shat did they sit on the loo with?

Lucky Beag was an alien as being on the small size Dorothy's weight did flatten him.

"I must have that alien," and was a whisper, who *whispered.*

"We must have that alien," *whose 'we'?*

"I must get rid of my cousins to better my chances of getting the alien," which cousin was *whispering?*

"I am so handsome Dorothy will lose the rest and run away with me, I can ditch her after our engagement party," a true PLUM *whispering* but who?

"I will convince Dorothy girls stick together and we drive away after mealtime after sticking a kitchen knife in all the tyres except our own of course," a feline *whisper,* besides, she owes me for the clean elastic I gave her with the hat and boots. Of course, there is only one girl here *so we can easily guess who this* is or perhaps one amongst these schemer dreamers wears frillies?

Did you think of that, some detective you are reader?

"Let us vamoose as I can see the law coming," Dorothy who could have easily said to Beag, "Bugger this lot, I will take you to our Earth Leader."

Or "I am Earth's Leader, let us go somewhere quiet and talk?"

"There are enemies of earth coming, use your mirror and destroy them Beag."

But like Susanna was a good girl.

"Hurry boys and girls crowd in the R.V, Wayne can drive," saying this to molly fears she would back stab them and 'bugger off with Beag.'

And that is why with shoving and pushing and pinching and real hard slapping in return for the pinching the lot of them got in the R.V.

Except Freckles and Jack, and that should have been a wake-up call?

If you was planning to double cross, you double cross but take the pets with you.

"Hey, where is Wayne?" Just takes one.

"In the driver's cab," takes another.

"Let me look," and much slapping as The Stooges crowded into the drivers cab.

"We been fooled," out of my way, and McSweeney took out his pistol and was to fire through the windscreen to screams from the others begging him not to.

Did he fire and shatter the windscreen covering those about him in unbreakable glass?

"You are some girl Dorothy," he said instead putting his pistol away and carelessly fired the weapon so Phillipo crawling at his feet screamed.

Was that Phillipo out of this tale of greed?

Remember police can shot you and get away with it? But was McSweeny a real police officer?

What was Philippo doing down there anyway?

He was about to cut the brake cables from this end and when the R.V. drove away jump out the small tight latrine window and drive away in his smashed battered delivery van.

Let us hope he could squeeze through the R.V. latrine window?

And Susanna got behind the wheel and drove off not amazingly fast as the tyres where all stabbed and flat.

"Quick the law is catching up, hit the gas girl," Diego panicking.

"We did better all go out and push so the R.V. will go faster," Ronaldo and opened the R.V. door and "Quick Stooges jump to it," and used to taking orders as hopeful unpaid film extras did.

Muck splashed them from the wheels.

Then the R.V. went down a ravine rather faster than The Stooges could run.

"Hey Mo, watch the rattler," Larry jumping.

"Get down," Mo as Curly Jo had jumped upon him, a wise move as the summer heat had brought the reptiles out.

And the police caught up but were smart folk, they heard the rattle of drums as the snakes did SAMBA, it was the heat, so did not go down the ravine but filled it with bullets for The Stooges were fugitives getting away from thirty-year sentences of hard labour.

And shot away the snakes.

How coinvent?

And for animal lovers, the snakes were extras, made of rubber.

And on the road below Dorothy levitated away this way and that as Beag was hugging a leg with these words, "LEG," and Wayne, he was more human so clung to the other leg with the word, "Lovely," as he was a Son of Adam with a wide grin.

"I will put up with Beag as will be mega rich at the end of this adventure," and looked down into the eyes of Wayne.

He waved a chef's hat at her.

"I can find a place in my huge kitchen in my newly bought mansion that once was owned by a film director.

I will remove his statue in the lawn and erect one of me," and looked at Beag whose eyes were large and belonged to a baby bear so added, "and one to Beag but not him," meaning Wayne.

And must get Jack off my elastics?

And the cat can stay sitting on my head.

Would Dorothy get away from the others and claim the reward for Beag all to herself?

Would she go 'All Motherly, invest in diapers and claim Beag as her son? No one had witnessed Beag use a latrine, so no one knew how he dumped?

Would she realise she was a wanted fugitive and spend the rest of her days making mail bags in a gaol?

Would she stop some whereas she was hungry. That raised the question, what did Beag it, and remembered horror films watched in the back of a car in a drive-in movie so remembered nothing.

But she did know one thing, Wayne had to be muzzled, her leg was going numb with him holding it so tight.

And she looked down into the chef's eyes that looked back all wide and tear filled as Wayne knew all about 'Puss and Boots.'

So broke Dorothy's soul so decided not to flick him off her leg and a good thing to, for they must be sixty feet up levitating. Speeding at forty.

Dorothy was a good girl.

And behind her if she did look, an abandoned R.V.

Abandoned, yes.
Look at those specs running across the farmland behind Dorothy puffing, sweating, panting and one was being carried.

"Puff wheeze pant," from McSweeney as he carried Susanna who knew all about men and how to get a lift.

"All I did was faint and gasp my last and the big dope picks me up and carries me
on his shoulders."

And a human snake is kicking and swearing in a field as his delivery van fell apart, but he did better run as all that hand waving and shouting has brought the occupants of the field to him.

"Moo," the filed occupants.

Now I do not know about you, but I do not trust cattle and they want revenge for turning them into burgers and smell 'the blood of a Philippine cousin in Phillipo, cousins that fried burgers.

"Moo," the cows.

Is that Phillipo sprinting towards the others.

Yes, it is and to make sure he went that way the thousand strong herd of revengeful cows behind him chased him.

Some shouts lie down and pretend to be dead and the animals chasing you will leave you alone.

Do you think this good advice?

"Mo," Larry jumping into Mo's arms.

What do you think tough Mo did?

Throw him off.

Yes, and slap him good.

Then struggle to breath as Curly Joe and Larry climbed all over him with these words, "MO, run there are cows coming."

And Mo threw them all off, looked and ran.

"Wait for us Mo," his friends and what else would they shout.

What about, "You," with a middle finger, "Plum," or, "wait till I tell your mum."

"Cow, where is my pistol?" Yes, it was McSweeny thinking of shooting all the thousand cows and when using the word, 'cow,' in front of a woman should have indicated animal cow and not human female.

Yes, a human female who felt insulted and you do not want to insult a human female having found something dangerous in her hands?

What was Susanna holding?

"You are looking for this handsome?" Susanna out to tease her NEW man in her life, well she liked the Tarzan types and his bicep staring her in the face were BIG, sweaty and his oxters needed a shower, how could she stand the smell?

Wake up Susanna he is no better than all the other men who did you wrong, he just wants one thing, a live in-house maid. Did you ask yourself what that rattling sound was?

It was his peanut brain rattling inside his head with all the running.

"Baby Doll, take your hand off the trigger?" McSweeney and awesome romantic music stuff was heard from breaks between the clouds, honest.

Was that heaven saying this relationship is blessed.

"Why," Susanna teasing or was she serious?

"Just do not squeeze the trigger Baby Doll," McSweeney.

"What like this?" Susanna liking to watch McSweeny's eyes fill with terror. *The big man was human.*

"Oh dear," Susanna as the pistol fired and what idiot keeps a loaded gun on him not on safety?

Who or what did Susanna shoot?

Was she facing the electric chair now?

Obviously, heaven had not blessed their relationship only McSweeney had.

And McSweeny clutched his bits as being all macho thought that did where a girl did seek revenge for calling her a cow.

So, he knew his mistake, **yes,** he had finish primary school and had ten fingers and ten toes to count with.

Where would you clutch, the chest where the expensive 'Austin Power' glue on red hairy chest was?

No, the moons where your kept the mobile in a back pocket.

The head in case the designer wig Mo wore was singed.

Your feet as that is where you kept the spare dollar in case Mo spent it on Mo.

See, McSweeny just checked out what was important to him.

And someone crawled out of the wrecked R.V.

"I am going back to making movies," the someone and hearing rattlers fled and ran into a police officer who handcuffed him.

"Release me, I am a famous film director."

"Yeh and I am Prince Harry," the police officer replied.

CHAPTER 8 EX TERRESTRIAL HIGHWAY

You might meet these chaps on Ex Terrestrial Highway

This is the highway that leads to 'Skin Walker Ranch,' as you do not live locally so would not know that. It goes from Las Vegas to Tonopah , Nevada.

It also illustrates how fast you can run if a thousand cattle are chasing you and you will cover ground faster.

Also, you will be fagged out.

And Ronaldo rested sitting on the cow he managed to sit upon. Well, he was a smart Philippine undocumented

immigrant on the make, so we did expect him to be smart.

And two Stooges got off Larry who was not as smart as Mo or Curley Joe who ended up carrying the other two. Do not worry, Larry was built squarely, and when two Stooges are slapping you carry, "YES SIR THREE BAGS FULL SIR."

And he held out a hand with a smile for a tip.

Do you know what he got?

Slap.

And McSweeney was puffed, Susanna had pointed his pistol at him, so he understood, 'Baby wants a lift,' and while she was up on his shoulders emptied his pistol. SMART GIRL, she by experience knew his types were as big as their loaded gun.

And where was Diego?

He took a bullet some careless girl had fired from a pistol.

Was he dead?

He better wish he were as Cousin Phillipo had found him.

Yes, that cousin who was crawling about the R.V. cab floor intent on cutting the brake cable.

And shows you he knew nothing about vehicles.

"Cousin Diego how nice to see you," the lying twerp thinking of MURDER.

Where was Diego shot that he could not keep up with the others?

A secret.

Bet you were not expecting that?

*

I am starving," Dorothy looking at Wayne in his chef uniform.

Wayne remembered Saucer Command and the alien general and swallowed, he had been away a year on the saucer, a lot of habits change on a planet, especially Earth in a year, was Dorothy a CANNIBAL? He watched films in Rest and Recreation, such as 'Earth Girls Eat Barbecued Aliens.'

"Hey fool, get a grip, Dorothy is an earth girl."

And was the wrong stuff to say, Earth Girls were easy was what flashed through Wayne's one-track mind. Fry them a greasy burger and give a wink and you were engaged hey presto.

But, that film, he did not want eaten so wanted to impress to live.

The next we land I will get Beag to rustle up an oven, olive oil, salt, pepper, and ingredients to make the winning Black Cherry Souffle with chocolate ice cream and a banana and chocolate stick stuck in the top, 'Smartie' eyes and mandarin orange slices as a mouth.

Sitting in a pond of vanilla custard with jellybean sharks swimming in the custard.

All covered in Mazapan chips for gluttons.

And Dorothy was a girl who watched her calories or took a laxative after a big meal.

She might not like ingredients.

Might be Jack and Freckles in there, he was a chef to an alien general who ate Earth easy girls?

Remember these terrible animal true mutilations at 'Skin Walker Ranch?' Aliens did it or SHAPE SHIFTERS.

Was Wayne involved, was he aboard the flying saucer seen above the cattle?

So, what then a cute dog called Jack and a calm cat wanting cuddles from an alien chef?

Dorothy might also be a diabetic.

Did Wayne ask her, of course not, he was a chauvinist who believed with such a dish Dorothy would always have him cook her meals **and marry him.**

Not if ingredients were any of the mentioned above.

Marry him, was he living in cuckoo land?

"Cuckoo," a reply.

"Beag take us down and feed me," Dorothy forgetting to specify feed her what?

Did aliens eat the product of insect farms?

Did they eat other inferior aliens on the evolutionary line?

Did all alien abductees return to earth or were they 'BAKED ALASKA?'

Or did Wayne practice his cooking for the alien general using missing persons.

If so, Wayne was a serial murderer and Dorothy better accidentally toss him over a shoulder towards those rubber rattlers.

But Wayne was small enough to cling to one of her legs leaving suction marks behind.

Was Wayne a HYBRID, did he have alien octopus genes, which would be telling.

A dirty minded fink of a hybrid more like it.

Just look at Beag, those big black shark eyes that told you nothing what he was thinking. He might be thinking of marrying LEG and dragging the rest of Dorothy behind in a suitcase wherever he went, to Mars, Fancy that peeking at the stars via little breathing holes in the suitcase?

It did be cramped in there with Jack and Freckles as Dorothy took her pets with her.

Wayne was an alien, right?

They think differently.

They eat our children.

Steal our jobs.

Move into lour houses.

How do I know all this, I read science fiction that is how I know.

And Beag landed on the side of a dusty empty road.

Empty because this was the famous Ex Terrestrial Highway to Area 51 and 'Skin Walker Ranch' where aliens thrive.

Also, Native American Monsters from their legends to terrify you away from the lost 'Dutch Man Gold Mine.'

And here was Dorothy, her pets and one alien, and one never mind, just call him Wayne.

And they came.

What came, is it a secret?

Yes, you will be told after an update on how the other alien seekers found Dorothy.

Here is Update

"Look Mo, balloons," Larry and was slapped because Mo liked to slap.

As for Larry he did not like being slapped but had this incredible urge to speak.

"Yeh Mo, we can ride in a balloon and catch up with Dorothy," Curly Jo and McSweeny puffed from carrying Susanna crashed into them.

Crashed?

Yes, he was a big man into protein drinks and weights and wanted 'Baby Doll' off his shoulders as her perfumes was fogging his mind so part of him was in a 'Land of Arabian Nights' were Susanna dressed in veils fed him exotic fruits that gave him the runs so spoilt his dream.

And crashing into the Stooges allowed him to slip her off him and onto them.

Did they notice Susanna was across their shoulders?

They were the Sons of Adam so that answers that.

And why was she there in the first place, she was the girl from next door, with a few binks of flash long eyelashes and a titter with a hand over her mouth, and that secret of girls from next door, how they manage to move the hem of the dress up when their hands are elsewhere.

The Stooges were smocks line hock and sinker.

And carrying Susanna ran into the nearest warm air balloon.

"Hey fools, this helium gas is alight, keep it up and we will be toast, thick toast like you," a skinny balloon controller appearing in the basket. Then he added looking up, "Owe, a girl is on my shoulders, Hello Baby just call me Handsome."

And explains why Susanna tightened her legs about his neck so he went blue.

Did she twist the legs so there was a loud CRACK, no that did be murder.

What a girl, what does she expect meeting men by jumping on their shoulders flashing pretty ankles?

To silence him she used a silent weapon all girls use, a silent stinky that made the balloon controller cross eyed.

And the Stooges climbed in and trod over the soft carpet that moaned.

"Baby Doll wait for me?" McSweeny holding out his hands to grab the balloon basket.

Now who in the basket flicked McSweeney's fingers away.

One less to divide the alien reward with.

And Susanna blew him a kiss but thought, "I am not a Baby Doll," for girls are allowed to have double standards.

And McSweeney investigated the three faces of The Stooges and since he was close, he got one, two and three slaps.

So, who flicked McSweeney's fingers away?

And a sweet voice drifted to his ears, "Go get your own balloon 'Big Boy.'" *And that is a clue to who flicked his fingers away.*

Mo sounds like a horse needing hot cough sucks.

Curley Joe sounds like a babble of children.

Larry sounds like a tape played backwards at speed.

That leaves Susanna with the sweet voice.

Maybe she could twist a neck, so you heard a loud CRACK, reward money was involved, There folks were forgivable, they had dreams that got nowhere. Susanna looking down into the dregs of a coffee cup in Diego's and The Stooges outside Diego's wanting in to eat greasy burgers but had no cash, extras like them were shot out of a cannon and landed so far away the movie set had packed up and left by the time they returned.

Yes, folk with broken dreams and now the alien had provided them with a get rich scheme, but first they had to,

1] Catch Beag.

2] Get rid of the other.

3] So only one was left.

4] Did that mean The Stooges thought of killing each other off so there were none?

"Help me up and I will help fly the balloon, just do not throw me over," and was a voice like an angel so was a sweet voice and was the balloon controller thinking terrorists had him and wished he had kept up his Life Insurance policy payments.

So might have been him that flicked McSweeny away.

And McSweeny huffed, puffed, and went red in the face and drew his pistol and fired.

But a smart girl earlier knew his type so had emptied the pistol.

"CLICK," went the chambers.

And instead of loading the pistol McSweeny in a rage threw it and knocked out the balloon controller.

What a throw, was his shattered dream he never made the grade as a base ball player but with the reward could buy his own 'Field of Dreams.'

And up and away went the balloon with three terrified occupants hugging each other, and a fourth who had driving lessons in a R.V. knew there must be a gas pedal, a break pedal, and a steering wheel.

"Have you looked for a handbrake Susanna?"

"R.V. never had one so why should s hot air balloon have one?" Susanna replies to our serious question.

They were going to heaven and hell soon readers.

And McSweeny saw Ronaldo leap from the back of a cow into a balloon and McSweeney said, "If he can do that so can I?"

But McSweeney was not standing on a cow for extra height so missed but did manage to grab a trailing rope attached to an anchor.

"PLUM" McSweeney hitting every cacti, sage brush, Shunk, rubber rattler, and square on into Phillipo being carried by Diego.

"Hurry Diego, I am bleeding out and the emergency is just over yonder," a lying cousin who knew being shot in an ear lobe added character, a hole for a large ear ornament, but not emergency, maybe pure 100% alcohol pored onto the wound as an antiseptic and the rest drunk.

So why did Phillipo convince Diego to carry him?

"I have been shot in the privates cousin Diego and need emergency so please carry me for my share of the alien reward

and what would your mother say?" A lying no good Phillipo who had wanted to cut the brakes in the R.V. when a gun was fired his way, so maybe he did need emergency.

Naw, more a lazy conman on the make and Diego a greedy fool.

And the next he knew he was lifted into the air as McSweeney wrapped his legs about him.

"Why?"

Was McSweeney practicing weightlifting on the lower anatomy?

"Crawl up over me fool and then pull me into the basket," McSweeny's answer explaining all.

And Renaissance Enlightenment entered Phillipo's mind.

"Eureka," he shouted and did exactly that and reached the basket.

"Goodbye Diego," he whispered Greed possessing him, and shook himself free of Diego.

"We are cousins," Diego knowing there was nothing between him and the soil below where stampeding cows waited for him.

But he was wrong, McSweeney caught him with his legs and held him.

"Grunt," McSweeney as Diego had spent years eating greasy hamburgers.

Now if only Susanna had seen his act of heroism, would she allow him to call her, "Baby Doll?"

But she was too busy fighting the controller of **her** balloon off her so was prompted to offer, "YES OFFER WHAT?"

A share in the alien reward if he could fly the balloon for her.

"And what if I do not?" The man asked and was slapped many times till his head was bobbing agreed.

He investigated the depths of the basket, there was The Stooges.

Yes, he did fly the balloon and capture the alien for himself. Greed had him.

He did also take the DOLL too as he was about to show the Air Force Hot Balloon flyers he could match their aerial display.

Oh, Good Grief, they were all about to die and all because there was a pretty ankle aboard ship.

He was truly a Son of Adam this stifling air man.

And someone offered him a share in an alien reward and did not mention a share in a prison.

"I am your man, I am your man," the warm air balloon controller full of the joys of spring and in his mind, "How do I get rid of these smocks, except Baby Doll," for he was a son of Adam. "I know, land for a relief session and while they are busy fly away. I know Baby Doll will be glad to be rid of them as means more presents from me to give her when I am in a good mood.

I will give her a poodle as a companion.

An electric cycle with a basket for the pooch to get about town when shops for me.

And money to buy new clothes from the charity shops.

And away in a dream was oblivious that Baby Doll was watching him fly the warm air balloon and had read his thoughts for females are good at that.

He was teaching her to fly a balloon.

"Just like driving the R.V.," she mused and noticed the hamper below in the depths of the basket.

These baskets are big.

And she kept giving the controller coffee to drink for she knew soon he must land and seek relief and Baby Doll did fly away without this Son of Adam.

"Wait for me," he did shout alerting Big Foot he was nearby, and Baby Doll did show a middle finger.

This was Skin Walker Ranch area, oh dear.

So, who was in the basket?

Time for a refresh.

Sussanne holding an empty thermos flask.

The controller with a big bladder.

The Stooges holding their tummies as the tummies were extended and bloated from eating everything in that basket.

The Stooges were greedy folk.

Did they offer their companions food or were they selfish BURKES.

Well, McSweeney was busy holding Phillipo close using bis fantastic mental powers to remember if Philippo was on the most wanted list, so ignored the obvious green sandwiches.

And Philippo was glad he was held aloft from the smelly green sauerkraut.

And Diego was whispering dreadful things to McSweeney such as, "My cousin is a wanted man back home for selling ferry tickets for a non-existent ferry, just throw him out Law Man," but did stuff his pockets full of rotten burgers that fell apert in your hand to offer McSweeney one as he interrogated Phillipo.

McSweeney was not daft, surely The Big Man did check what he was stuffing into his mouth, or would he, it would taste just like a greasy roadside burger, delicious.

GREED HAD TURNED TO MURDEROUS THOUGHTS BUT NOT DEEDS YET.

Can we count the film director as demised?

No, when he promised parts in his latest Napoleonic film he was let go after a donation to a Police Charity of course. So be happy he was free, and we will get to go to the cinema to watch his film, "Dracula meets Napoleon."

CHAPTER 9 SAUCER COMMAND AGAIN

30 fried rubber courses, Wayne was a vegetarian and knew the aliens ate anything.

"My general what can we do about the food being served these days?" A brave aspiring officer abord ship.

All the aliens knew it was the general's fault by freeing Wayne, now they had to eat Spaceship Field Rations.

Corned something that still had tentacles hanging from the sides.

Not to mention the watery mash where eyeballs blinked at you.

And tepid water full of floating algae to wash it down.

Yes, the crew aboard ship blamed the general, rebellion was in the air.

How do aliens rebel, just like us.

First, they stuff the general full of food laced with sleeping pills and when he awakes, he is in the cooler.

Who is at the ship's wheel.

That aspirer mentioned earlier.

But rebellion was not here yet and the general had to act quick.

He needed Wayne back.

"Officer take control of the kitchens, we all expect a fine dinner," was the general's attempt at getting Wayne back, he was shifting the buck yes, he was.

Anyway, not to let Wayne free did give alien abductions a bad name. Then who wanted to come back to earth, it was rumoured all night parties were all the bash on Planet Mars.

CHAPTER 10
MONSTERS

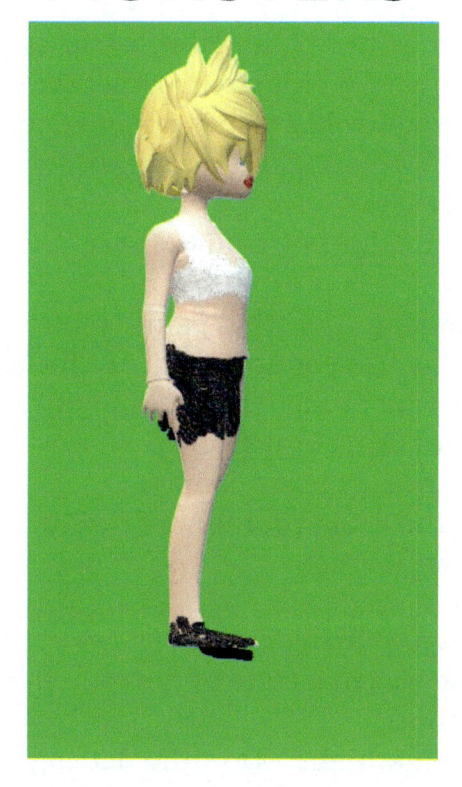

"Look there they are?" Susanna excited at seeing Dorothy and the aliens again.

The controller peered over the balloon basket as he was a curious fellow and you know what they say, "Curiosity killed the cat."

"Big Foot, them, they are the aliens?" He was disappointed as no one had bragged about a Big Foot reward.

"No Mister, look closer, see there is Dorothy in her red shoes, the little man is a munchkin, and the other is the alien.

"Ah, Dorothy," and said it implying Susanna was no longer Baby Doll, but that did not matter as she helped him to get a closer look at those below on the road.

She flipped him over the basket. "One, two, three, out," she went flippantly.

"Baby Doll why? I had plans for you," the controller shouting up pulling his rip cord on his small parachute on his rump.

See, a balloon controller comes prepared for the worst.

Mr. Controller what about the passengers?

"What about them?"

"Never call me Baby Doll again Mister," Susanna called back to him.

My, Susanna and Dorothy paint a picture of American Womanhood as a free-living breed of chickens independent from those that want to cage them, resilient, career minded, full of True Grit with a Gun Ho attitude.

The controller never had a chance.

"Wayne, are those Big Foot we are meeting?" Dorothy asked Wayne as he spoke English.

"Hiss," Freckles putting out her claws so Wayne could not answer her as he was in a state of nervous shock from possible exposure to tetanus.

"Beag, do something?" Dorothy letting down American Womanhood.

"LEG," Beag replied illustrating a point why Dorothy had asked Wayne for advice.

Not to worry Jack ran ahead, stopped, barked, lifted a leg, and ran back to hide behind Dorothy.

"Yummy," one Big Foot number 1 speaking English.

"Why are you here?" Another number 2.

"You are monkeys so how can you speak English?" Dorothy.

"Monkeys, where, oh him," number 3 and picked Wayne up by the head as the ape's hand was so big it covered Wayne's lugs.

"We were visited by missionaries who taught us English and then we invited them to dinner," another MONKEY number 2 again.

Dorothy did what any sensible woman did do, she shook Beag with these words, "Do something?"

And Beag's mirror flew up to Dorothy and said, "Everything is under control, relax kiddo."

"Beag, is that you?" Big Foot number 1 taking Beag away from Dorothy.

"Dorothy," Beag holding a handout to her.

"You know Beag?" Dorothy.

"This is Skin Walker Ranch lady, what did you expect to see here, shape shifters?" Big Foot number 3 and began to howl and

his eyes glowed RED.

Was he a shape shifter? That would explain how the Big Foot appear and vanish just like that. And you can bet that the shape shifters smell bad also as are not house trained, so they must be Big Foot as is told they stink?

"Wayne can cook?" Number 2 and held Wayner upside down by a foot.

"Oh dear, cook what, Wayne?"

And mirror flew over to this number 2, so it saw its reflection in mirror and howled in horror. It was ugly so threw Wayne into the air to cover its eyes so it would not have to look at itself.

"Help," Wayne not liking his chances of not landing on a hard rock.

"Wee," Beag off to catch his friend as Beag *was a good alien, not like the ones out of 'Mars Attack.'*

"Missed," Dorothy cringing as Wayne landed on a hard rock. That was some landing, Beag better do some healing as Wayne looked cross eyed and happy as he watched prepared food on platters spin round his head.

Who would save Dorothy from a fate worse than death?

What horrid fate, these whatever monsters had only been

making small chit chat?

Because monsters always run away with the milk maid and tie her over a railway line till, she agrees to marry.

Wow is that Dorothy's fate.

"Hello girl," and was Susanna so Dorothy had some explaining to do.

"Yeh, where did you get the monkey suits from," the film director, he here too?" Mo and slapped a monkey number 1 on the moon. "Stunt folk you promised part of the alien reward?" Curly Jo slapping number 2 places as everything was covered in dense fur.

"Yeh, if there are monkeys there must be peanuts, cough up monkey," Larry throttling the right knee of number 3.

"Who are these fools?" Number 4 asked.

"We are The Stooges," The Stooges chorused just before they were torn to shreds.

Torn to shreds?

Yes, what do you think these monsters did do, laugh, they were monsters and monsters tear to shreds all right?

And the monsters laughed.

Not The Stooges though.

"Dorothy you better hand Beag over to us if you want any help?" McSweeney patting his shoulder holster no longer wanting to be friends with Dorothy, and if we could sneak in through ear wax into his brain, we did hear him think, "I will get Beag to levitate me to a news station and claim the reward," but he had been away from Beag too long so did not know Beag virtually spoke one word, "LEG."

"Shave your legs McSweeny."

"Dorothy, I will always help you, what do you want me to do?" Diego.

"Drop dead," Dorothy replied.

"Dorothy, quick jump into the balloon and we can fly away together to safety," Ronaldo for the moment giving up Beag and being content with the second prize, Dorothy.

"Drop dead," Dorothy louder.

"I will offer these creatures the remains of the hamper food and when they fall down with colic, we can all escape," Philippo thinking of dividing shares out at a higher altitude.

MURDER was on his mind.

There where a lot of hard rocks lying about, just ask Wayne how hard they were?

Then the sirens sounded, the helicopters whirred, and a loudspeaker blared, "This is Government Restricted Property, hands up or else," and the click and loading of a thousand shot guns was heard.

"Gulp," three times followed by slapping.

And the savage furry creatures turned into Men in Black under dark glasses.

"How is that possible?" Dorothy.

"I must get one of those dark glasses and look cool," McSweeney.

And McSweeny reached for a pair on a man in Black, who responded by pretending to put them on McSweeny's ears, but poked McSweeny's eyes instead with the legs.

"I am blinded," and "that was so painful."

"We must find out how that illusion trick was done, and we will always be employed and fed," Mo meaning he must have the illusionist secret. That mean he would not share the rations, of course not, he did share his last bread crumb with his friends for

he was that sort of guy and because he was looking for a way to divide the last bread crumb a pigeon flew down and gobbled it up.

He was an animal lover too.

"Dorothy, we got to help each other, you have no idea what it is like to be the only 'BABY DOLL' here," Susanna and Dorothy looked at her with understanding and nodded feeling ashamed for her mother had brought her up to change her underwear daily so was a good girl.

"Baby Dolls will come with us," the Men in Black.

"See what I mean?" Susanna.

And the Men in Black herded Phillipo, Diego, and Ronaldo into a group.

"Hey, we are boys, they are girls," Phillipo out to save his skin.

And a Man in Black showed these guys a wanted poster of them.

"No one will miss you," and this Man in Black sounded like shape shifter number 1.

"We have busted our clean records for an alien reward to get rich when riches were amongst us all the time," Susanna wisely.

Was the girl learning?

"Beag come here," the loudspeaker.

"Dorothy it is my general, I want to stay with you," Beag.

"Owe," Susanna remembering all the broken engagements, so saw Beag and Dorothy in a suburban house with kids and pets and a washing line full of diapers.

But what could they do against all these Federal Agents skimming down ropes from the helicopters?

Sweet nothing folks.

They were outnumbered.

"Mirror?" Beag.

Not a whimper, it was playing dead.

And the Highway Patrol caught them up at last.

"These are our fugitives," and to enforce that handcuffed our greedy adventurers.

And separated the girls from the men.

And left Phillipo, Diego and Ronaldo with The Men in Black, there was something strange about these men, fur was protruding from the ends of their trousers and jackets.

That is why Freckles and Jack with animal sense left them alone, *they were focused and knew humans did not have furry hands.*

"I demand United States Justice," Phillipo seeing the fur too.

Then one of the men in Black lifted a leg and scratched the

back of an ear.

Phillipo fell to his knees begging mercy, praying loudly, and inching away on those knees.

He got several feet away before a Man in Black lept in front of him, picked him up by the hair and carried him back.

"They are all coming with me," it was the loud voice from the loudspeaker again.

"It is my general Dorothy," Beag.

Phillipo hobbled away quickly to the rest of the of the men, turned and gave a middle finger to the strange furry Men in black.

What Men in Black, they had vamoosed, gone, vanished just like Men in Black do.

At your front door one moment warning you to secrecy about anything you saw, then gone, as if they were never there except left calling cards, *"You will regret telling what you saw."*

This is all part of Area 51, 52, 53, where aliens are entertained.

A place where aliens were dissected.

A place where even presidents did not know existed.

So why was the general not dissected?

He was big, and his flying saucer was bigger, and the weapons bigger and that explains that.

"Cooking tonight are we Wayne? My human counterpart is waiting with excitement at what you can cook WAYNE," the general.

Human counterpart?

"A thirty-course alien galaxy menu," Wayne knowing that did take all night and the eaters be full after meal five and he could stop cooking, yes, Wayne was a smart chef all right.

He was smarter, he used microwaves and many dishwasher, abductees from planets.

Perhaps the nagging mother-in-law, happy now?

No, the nagging father-in-law, that better?

Wayne was using his NOG, Gods gift to all, even him.

So, folks men and women, as employment here was not discriminatory, rounded up our gang and gave them seats next to windows in a grey prison bus so they could look out with furlong looks to break a heart.

Highway patrol motorbikes straight out of the television series were to be escorts, blue lights flashing, sirens honking, handsome film stars stuffed down patrol unbuttoned shirts and riding trousers already to burst and reveal more than the white vests.

Exciting yes, and they wore dark glasses and polished up black boots.

And the general entered the bus.

"Halo," what else did you expect him or her to say, "Seig Heil General," or "Wet your pants have we?" "Tough lot are we, well we will soon beat that out of you?" "Hungry are we, so am I and Wayne will cook up something for me, did I forget to tell us?"

And the prison bus driver started the engine and the bus jumped away.

"Whose driving?" The general and the driver popped HER head out of the drivers cabin.

It was Susanna.

"How?" The general asked just as Dorothy jumped him and did a Kug Fu work out on him.

Bet that hurt Dorothy.

Why because earth gravity made the general spongy, bouncy and squeezy.

"I am puffed," Dorothy collapsing in a heap.

"But not us," and The Stooges jumped the general, misjudged their leap, fell upon Dorothy, and worked out.

Not a slap went down.

But notice Dorothy's face going red with anger, these three funny men were DEAD when Dorohty recovered.

DEAD do you hear me?

And Susanna having pledged that girls stay together slammed on the brakes.

My did the Stooges fly and cover the front windscreen making funny faces there.

Why Mr. Mo was cross eyed.

Curly Joe also but with an added mouth gape and tongue out.

And Larry was awake as his body woke insolating him from the WHACK of contact with the windscreen, see he was overweight.

And because of his weight he was first to slide to the bus floor.

And looked up at the GENERAL.

"Titter," Larry tittered.

Never mind Beag came to the rescue, of his general, why because he was a crawling alien twerp.

"My leader, these humans have been chasing me, can we vaporise them?" Beag telling the truth and why to The Stooges he was a twerp.

"Hey Beag, we are best friends," Phillipo lying as he was an aspiring liar to be recorded in the Guinness Book of records.

"He is the leader of us, vaporise him," Diego and Ronaldo together seeing a way to vaporise Phillipo's reward share.

They did tell his mother he volunteered to be a Martian settler of N.A.S.A.

And McSweeny went for his gun for he was full of True Grit and Gun Ho John Wayne Spirit and should have checked to see if

the Highway patrol did leave a loaded gun on him, of course not, and who ever took it had a sense of humour, they stuck a rubber Gia Monster in the holster.

A GIA MONSTER?

McSweeny hated Gia Monsters so screaming threw it away, so it landed on the general who beat it blue but to do so beat himself up blue as the rubber lizard fell down his torso.

He beat places so explains the funny faces girl readers.

And Susanna drove with her foot right down on the gas

pedal.

Did she know where she was going.

What woman driver does?

And the yellow prison bus was escorted by motorbikes of The Highway Patrol.

At 80 m.p.h. that school yellow bus covered many miles in fifteen minutes.

If you are wondering why a school bus was used, well, there were no grey [prison buses available and yellow is a nice bright colour.

"Mirror where are we going?" Beag asked.

And because it was Beag asking and the general was rubbing alien anti inflammatory cream onto his body where he had beaten it blue, Beag was now brave and fearless.

"Look ahead and read the ranch sign," Mirror.

And Beag looked ahead and forgot he could read English thanks to a language implant that relied on an alien back on the saucer to send it translations, and because the general was

absent this alien was partying, blowing streamers, drinking fizzy drink, and eating pizza just like a human.

None were forth coming, since without Wayne's cooking standards had fallen in saucer command kitchens, other aliens were on the throne busy.

Only aliens sighs and moans and the continued rustle of toilet paper heard.

"I must get Wayne back, we just eat greasy burgers covered in mayo, argh, my moons," and was the general in the common latrine aboard bus as he would never have made it back to his gold-plated private loo with each paper square showing the face of his emperor imprinted.

Yes, he loved his emperor, and the new chef was an aspiring cousin who knew with the general indisposed he was free to take over the spaceship, dream on aspirer. He was now chef; he had a duty to sup his gravies to see if the arsenic could be tasted.

Well, he had eaten his own food so was indisposed as well.

But for us, we humans not in the prison bus the ranch sign

said, **CAN YOU GUESS?**

"Welcome to Orlando Disney World," believe me?

It said, "Skin Walker Ranch, Enter at Own peril."

And Susanna did not stop as she forgot where the brake was, well what was this driving lesson number four or three?

So demolished a bunk house. Perhaps the one they were to sleep in.

'Girls Dormitory,' a sign above where the front door had been.

And Susanna remembered the hand brake so yanked it on, so the bus stopped right on top of the handy back door exit.

We know this as a sign lay under the bus.

'Handy Back Door exit,' it read.

The back emergency exit window opened as the Highway patrol do things different.

"Out you come, chow time at the Skin Walker Ranch," and those inside shuffled towards the speaker holding their stomachs as Susanna had been driving recklessly as SHE WAS A LEARNER WOMAN DIRIVER and thus make the best ambulance drivers ever.

"Then will dissect you," obvious this law officer had a sense of humour but not those he addressed as he or she was met with retching noises.

Susanna had been driving.

And the general got to the exit, but he was bigger than the exit even after visiting the latrine.

"A fatty we got a fat one," a tough police itching to be tough so whacked the generals legs, so he collapsed.

"Do you know who you just hit?"

"No, whisper me then?"

And he who had used his baton put the baton into the hands of the first bus passenger getting out.

It was Phillipo.

Who being quick minded as was a villain hid it down his

trousers, so it gave him a stiff walk.

Never mind, the general would have all frisked.

Does that mean this low-down person who wanted to murder is written out by being sent to an alien penal colony on Planet Dog in the Milky Way?

Not likely, this story needs a low-down villain to match the goodness in Beag who shines light out of his never mind.

"We girls need a bath," Dorothy sticking together with the girls.

Well, they had sweated FEAR as Sussan had been speeding calling out, "How do you veto freedom and safety.

Safety, were they really going to squeeze out a bus window and blow away in the bus Jetstream at 100 m.p.h.?

Then with all that retching sounds yes baths were needed.

And the girls were led away to a bunk house not demolished by a learner driver.

'Male Dormitory,' a sign over the front door read.

"What about us?" Diego asked.

A towel was thrown, and a law officer's finger pointed at a horse trough.

They were men, not girls, so were made of nails, Gia Monsters, and True Grit.

Then the finger pointed to an outhouse where buzzing was heard.

"I am a lawman myself, look here is my badge and I.D. in my wallet," McSweeny who panicked as he rummaged for them.

There were thieves amongst the adventurers, **can you think who they might be?**

"Yeh and I am Daffy Duck," the officer and stuck his magnum under McSweeney's nose.

Did McSweeny think that it was about time to stop playing with guns, they might hurt you?

"I must buy a bigger Magnum when out of this mess back in San Diego," McSweeney.

*

"With this real law enforcement I.D. and badge, I can get first class treatment here, be fed well, steal a helicopter and be away with Beag stuffed in an overnight zip up bag," the thief.

Sounds familiar.

And how did he plan to get hold of Beag?

"I will lay a trail of 'Gummy Bears to me where I will be waiting with a large butterfly net and I will have him," surely the mind of a desperate individual who had lost it somewhere topside, and who would not loose it mentally with what these folks had gone through and knew thy faced if caught, Alcatraz, that haunted prison vacant of humans but not spooks.

They say Al Capone is still there.

And Diego read his mind as he was his cousin, "The alien general will send Phillipo to Plant Neptune, and I will make sure he goes because I am a way to tell the general what Phillipo is planning.

Gummy Bears, no lay a trail of cookies bought from those visiting Brownies over there, what, Brownies here, By Planet Jupiter they get about?" Thus, having lost his mental stability and if we looked closer, he was eating 'Gummy Bears.'

"Children, to think I am relayed to them," Ronaldo and moved towards the bunk house where the girls were.

Oh, yes?

It was Beag that stopped him on his way to see Dorothy and introduce LEG to his general and then be vaporised maybe?

"Hey what the?" Ronaldo as he was lifted into the air and just like that photographers in military pressed uniforms appeared with cameras filming.

"You are one of them that chased MY Dorothy," Beag and Ronaldo ignored MY for he was full of himself.

Dorothy could only belong to him, of course after he gave her a stolen bag of Gummy Bears. What is it with these Gummy Bears. Well, they are nice children's sweeties.

And Ronaldo gave Beag the bad and Beag ate them and liked

them so much he forgot he was holding something heavy.

What do you do when you are holding a heavy dead weight, well, drop it and that he did.

Onto photographers so they broke his fall so only filled his pants in terror for he thought he was a thousand feet up when he was only twenty.

"Beag," Dorothy letting her alien into the bunk house, "this is Susanna."

"A bad LEG," Beag knowing who Susanna was.

"Is he some sort of pervert?" Susanna asking to be what? No idea what angry aliens do to silly humans that just do not know when to keep quiet.

For an instant Dorothy thought of buttering her side of the toast with jam and agreeing. Now remember Dorothy was changing her spots and had been brought up by her mother to change her underwear daily, so said, "No, this is Susanna who is with me now."

That is not what I would have said, oh I did have blamed Susanna till the cow jumped over the moon to make sure I got her share of the alien reward.

GREED had infected me rom these folk. Like a flea full plague, it jumped from them to me and from me to you reader.

Anyway.

"My General has invited you to dinner Dorothy," and Beag looked at Susanna and noticed she had two LEGS.

Nice and shapely.

What gives with this alien?

Dorothy sighed and being a good girl did not insist Susanna wear trousers from now on. There could only be her legs to be called LEG and worshipped by Beag and Dorothy already knew it was her legs thanks to shaving cream, hair remover and ladies razors.

Perhaps Beag needed spectacles, or he failed his anatomy class which we were told he came last in exams remember and so thought that is where humans lept their brains.

In legs?

Remember he was an alien.

Did we just catch him grinning g like Wayne.

Have you met an alien?

No, then I could ne correct.

And Beag grew his mirror to an enormous size for the girls to balance precariously on as it flew them towards the ranch house.

Where was Beag?

Guess?

"LEGS," was heard as he wrapped about four legs.

This cute little alien knew his business.

*

"Look boys, we must overpower our guards and steal Beag and a truck, drive through the gates and speed to San Diego," McSweeny thinking and added, "Baby Doll, I will miss you."

How nice of him?

"I like Susanna, she can drive, I seen her, but I do not know if you can," Larry feeling safe as he had Mo and Curly Jo next to him, had next to him as they were thinking too and could see the R.V. passengers.

Men in Black, alien men in Black blowing balloons from bubble gum and letting it burst over their faces, then a forked tongue darted out from fake red rubber lips and licked it all away.

McSweeney admired the handguns in the holsters.

They seemed bigger than the magnum he was to buy.

They were sawn off assault rifles and machine guns.

McSweeny would have to save hard to buy one, much better to steal one as they made their escape with Beag to San Diego.

Do you think McSweeny did still in one piece after overpowering his alien guards.

He did send the Stooges in first to soften the enemy up.

Then trod over the boys and odds that had been The Stooges and somersault on the guards and knock them all over, knock one and that guard topples into the next and the next till all down just like ten pin balling that McSweeny was no good at.

But McSweeny was full of confidence, they were aliens, so The Stooges had nothing to fear.

Did McSweeny plan to ask The Stooges if they wanted this mission?

And from a pocket McSweeney took a clay pipe and sucked on it, and said to the guards, "I will return," as he had nagging doubts about the success of his escape plan.

CHAPTER 11 THE LAST SUPPER

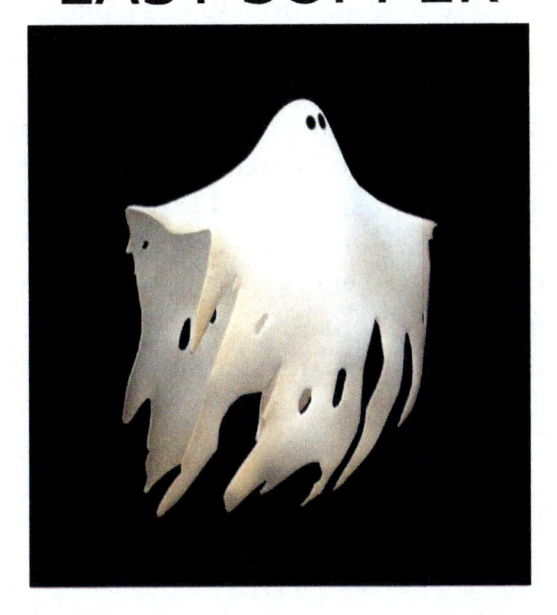

The meal inside the Skin WLKER RANCH House was huge, from the outside it was a normal ranch house with a set of long horn skulls above the main doorway.

Another skull looked like a giant apes.
There were four empty wooden shields.
Mo, Curly Jo, Larry and McSweeny as written on them.

If one looked closer you did see a stamp on the top of the skulls, 'Made in Ohio Plastic Joke Factory,' remember this was Skin Walker Ranch home to strange happenings, and those plastic skulls were the start.
A grand piano was in the entrance way.

On closer inspection if you lifted the lid, you did see all the keys removed. Yes, strange it was under the piano.

A giant wind-up key was under the piano.

Three blind mice with canes were encouraging three pigs to keep the key wound up.

Chopin's 'Funeral March' was playing, but who was playing, you could see the keys moving, the place was haunted.

Here is a clue, as each key sounded inside the piano squeaks were heard.

Stuffed antelope parts littered the walls. It was disgusting until you stood on a chair and looked closer, "Hey folks, they are not stuffed antelopes, but stuffed teddy bears so old the stuffing is loose. Yes, teddy bears with parts missing, such as the glass eyeballs now in a glass beaker on the grand piano watching you enter this strange ranch house.

Glass tanks of living corn snakes and rubber Gia Monsters were on wooden units.

Most folk were afraid of snakes so never got close to check if they were deadly rattlers and the Gia Monsters RUBBER.

Bag pipes hung from a wall nail.

Bag pipes?

Yes, someone here had red hair, Celtic ancestry and to prove it, now and again the wail of bag pipes heard.

The biggest painting was of a naked woman and her eyes followed you because someone else was behind the painting watching you. Shame, the subject matter was sitting on a chair holding a glass water jug that distorted the subject matter, on purpose so you did not notice the eyes watching you or smell the cigarette smoke drifting from the eyes.

The watcher obviously a smoker asking for lung disease.

'Public toilets,' on a sign above two doors and on each door a lock opened with the deposit of a dollar coin ten times.

The owner knew toilet paper was expensive and so was a cleaner, so folks were encouraged to run outside and check the grass before showing moons in case of meeting snakes and Gia

Monsters.

This place had atmosphere.

Vultures lined the roof wanting to meet you, DEAD.

Wonder of wonders, then the men folk were shown into a dinning room the size of a basketball pitch, twenty-eight by fifteen metres, by golly that is a big eatery.

Jealousy filled Diego's soul.

"Not as big as my eatery," Diego so all got behind him as he was suddenly expendable.

There sat at the top a human, on cushions to make him look bigger. On his right shoulder a house-trained parrot, it had a small diaper on.

The human wore a golfers cap, it had been red but was now white.

At the lower end of the LONG dinning table sat the general in a big chair as he was a big alien and got that way as Wayne's cooking deserved eaten to the last crumb on the last plate of a twenty-course meal.

If nothing else, Wayne could cook.

On the generals lap a Gia Monster from Planet Dog, and it was not rubber, it also had a collar embedded with gold coins with a face of the aliens' emperor on them, just to remind the general whose Boss.

Well, if alien life could evolve in the Milky Way, why not rubber Gia Monsters.

Beag and the girls sat next to him as did alien junior officers and one of them was aspiring to take over the generals job, *remember him from the 'Saucer Command earlier chapter.'*

And he had not taken over yet, he was being cautious, he wanted to live a bit longer. He was just getting over colic from eating greasy alien burgers.

And humans in suits and others in uniforms with rows of medals and others in laboratory white gowns sat at the table.

"Squeak," from one of the pockets of these scientists. A white mouse appeared at the top of a pocket, *"OH Sweet Jesus, it* had three heads, each with dark glasses and a paw appeared, it held a white cane."

Now strange colly wobble sounds and a fair ground organ blasted, taped disturbed bird sounds heard, see, the place had a strange eerie atmosphere.

Was it haunted by blond, white mice?

This was Skin Walker Ranch.

Then a monkey under the long table humped Phillipo's legs.

Because the monkey knew Phillipo was a villain and, in this tale, bad guys get karma.

And the water jars on the table near the scientists had teddy bear eyeballs floating in them. Good grief, was this place a forgotten Holly Wood Prop?

A quick look at the walls will answer that.

There were black and white pictures of Abbot and Costello, Charlie Chaplin, The Three Stooges, Bela Lugosi, Boris Karloff, Shrek, and Rip Van Winkle.

That answers that.

And the men passengers were not seated next to Dorothy and Susanna but the human and alien scientists, did we neglect to mention that science here was a shared effort, the aliens learning about us through alien abductions and never mind, and the humans learning new weapons of mass destruction from the aliens.

And Wayne walked in followed by waiters, human and alien, and Wayne stood aside as the waiters filled the long table with aroma.

There was much noise from talk and eating so no one noticed Diego choke as the monkey below the table stretched a hand up to steal what was on his plate. Would you choke if furry fingers appeared from between your legs where important thingmabobs were kept? What must have gone through Diego's mind.

Was he worried something would appear in a glass jar for public viewing?

"What have I eaten has caused this growth places," his reason not to worry.

And the girls noticed and gave him sour glances.

They would never sit next to him again, not that they did anyway, but they now had a legal reason.

So, he panicked all right till the monkey stuck its face up and seeing no food offered to it, bit places so Diego swooned, and the monkey chatted away to Ronaldo who gave the monkey fruit from a bowl.

Wise man.

The monkey refused that and took his roast.

The scientists fed their monkeys here a good, varied diet.

It was rumoured that the Chupacabra those vampire dogs were reared here as a secret weapon to let loose in the sewers of our enemy cities. Yep, you can just imagine Putin on the throne and one of them emerges.

"So Beag, what progress have you made to meet the Earth Leader?" The alien general asked.

Beag tittered and roughly upended Dorothy and showed his general a LEG.

"But you already know the earth leader so why Beag was sent here?" A brave mirror wanting to be pieces in glass beakers.

And to prove a point a giant screen slid down a wall and the anthem of The United States was played.

There stood a man leaning on a golf club.

"Where is the experiment?" This new human asked.

"Beag stand up," the general ordered, and the cute little alien did.

Maniacal laughter came from the golf player.

"If you want any more cash from the taxpayers I want

to see a real super hybrid, one that is handsome, a pin up for the ladies, biceps that can shell nuts, legs that can outrun my racehorses, whoopsie, never declared them, retracted, in other words, value for money," the golfer and went on to putt his ball and missed, never mind, a baboon under a red hat that read,

'MAKE AMERICA GREAT,' and in bright striped shorts of the U.S.A flag, darted out from an electric golf buggy and plunked the ball down the hole.

It wore white 'Y' fronts to cover that mass of pink baboon moons.

This is a children's tale so the rules of decency

must be observed.

As it darted back to the buggy it somersaulted to gobble a peanut flicked in the air by the golfer.

A rip was heard in the white 'Y' where red moons En mass showed.

Horrid it be.

"I am not impressed either," the general looking at Beag floating in the air, NAKED,

almost ladies as he had a willy warmer on shaped as TED.

This is a decent story void of nudity.

And on another screen that had silently slid down a wall, the figure of an alien under a crown, sweating under a sable robe that 'French

Emperors' wore.

"Beag, what can you do?" This alien royal having already decided Beag's fate.

So Beag tap danced between the dishes on the table and splashed in them where the male passengers sat.

Something tells us he did not like the passengers.

Something alive with tentacles clung to Phillipo, why, because karma was here.
"The troops on Dog Planet can do with an entertainer," the royal alien and "chef."

Now a lot of chat went on between the golfer and this royal alien that we are not interested in, such as how to win elections, conquer planets, give everyone a mind set that worships you and to donate what they own to your cause, by giving everyone a game console so they become blank beings.

"LEG," Beag cried as alien guards dressed as classical Roman legions took him away.
Dorothy felt a tear coming on, she was the good girl from next door out of 'Spider Man.'
Was she crying for Beag or the fact all the effort to keep Beag burned off unwanted calories, tears of joy reader.
Susanna let go two tears as she was used to crying over

a broken heart, hers. What was Beag to her, a passport to a better life independent of those that saw her as a 'Baby Doll.'

McSweeny.

You know, she had the brains to realizes

without Beag she did never have learned to drive. *Eh, hold on Susanna how many lessons did you have, and much white hair did your passengers grow?* She was grateful to the little alien and sad to see him go, he had provided her an adventure.

Was she true, how do you cry over an alien that looks like something out of 'The Lord of The Rings?' But her mother had taught her to change her elastics daily too so must be a good girl capable of real emotions.

"No one takes an alien from me," McSweeney planning Beag's escape.
So, what have you planned McSweeney? Nothing yet, all right we will tap your head later with a hammer so you hear us. Us being we readers.

And six tears rolled forth from The stooges as the girls were affecting them. Had their mothers taught them to change their smalls daily also. Were they good men then or were they crying as they saw Beag as a new member of their acting troop depart.

Mo saw Beag as his flying mount about circus rings encouraging clapping and coin throwing as Curly Jo led a blind folded elephant across stepping stones where Larry was tied.

And the crowd did go wild, and the elephant did run out the exit flap taking the big tent down.

And not a tear fell from Phillipo as he was the villain and

thinking of ways to steal Beag and teach him to work for him stealing from bank safes and such.

"He should be grateful to me, his mug shot did be on all televisions. As soon as he levitated folks did report him and sirens galore and thanks to his mirror, a bullet proof shield in operation.

Why I did buy a Phillipo mobile ten times larger than 'Bat Man's' Bat mobile, and Flames, not exhaust to deter following Highway Patrol motorcycles. Yes, a handsome villain like me thinks of everything.

Moriarty did be proud of me; he did have a signed picture of me in his lounge wall in heaven.

I did even dress Beag in a tight-fitting alien costume.
Dream on Phillipo.
See, Phillipo's mother had not taught him to change his shorts daily so must be a bad boy and
a smelly one.

Ronaldo pretended to wipe tears away from the back of his hands as he watched what was going on, absorbing details of escape with Beag and Dorothy, or Susana, he was not greedy and he did not change his smalls daily and all this exertion and fear producing 'skid marks' had made him a powerful smelly boy.

Diego bit his lip so shed lots of tears making sure Dorothy saw him, he knew Beag was out of reach and Dorothy was madly in love with him, Susanna also, mirror maybe.

And he smelled and was the fault of all this running about and being a chef who provides colic to his customers, yes, he did not wash his hands after a dump and wiped them on his apron and smalls and dried them on the burgers you were to eat with this song, "Rub a dub, a dub, three men in a tub."

His mother was ashamed, "He escaped from an orphanage, he is not mine," she protested from the Philippines LYING.

The film director was filming everything from a ring and was shedding tears of joy as the film did pay for the cast of that Napoleonic film he was making back there and more, a divorce and a new wife, perhaps Dorothy and Susanna.

They were all human passengers apart from two. Freckles and Jack knew wrong was going down, animals did.

That is why they ran ahead of the alien guard to greet them later.

"I have a plan now," Mcsweeny thinking he did let the pets do the messy work of freeing Beag.

"So do I," Dorothy thinking of letting Beag do the messy work of freeing himself.

"Yes, me too," Susanna thinking of letting McSweeny do the messy work of freeing Beag.

"Slap, slap" I am thinking Mo so was not thinking.

"I will let Diego rescue Beag then steal the alien from him, yes, a brilliant idea, how I will whack him on the head with a handy Gia monster as they are everywhere," Phillipo showing criminal creativity.

"I will wait till Diego steals Diego from Phillipo then steal the alien from him, how, I will whack him on the head with two Gia Monsters as I have two hands, a wonderful idea," Ronaldo showing how smart he was.

"I will wait till my cousins are incapable of intellect from Gia Monster bites then, "They can have Beag, it is Dorothy I will steal and Beag will follow her," Diego being Brilliant, *"but how will you steal Dorothy who beat you blue last time?"* And Diego huffed and puffed thinking hard and consoled himself by sucking a thumb.

"Why is my cousin sucking a thumb?" Ronaldo and held his breathe in frustration as his idea frizzled out, so went blue and passed out.

"A man like me never turns his nose up at opportunity knocking," Phillipo and frisked the unconscious Ronaldo, in front of horrified spectators
"He is not one of us," they chorused.

"I want to hire that man as my new caddie," the golfer and from nowhere a golf ball came from

the screen and hit Phillipo square on.

"Tweet, chirp, tweet," a man like Phillipo tweeted seeing circling birds about his head.

And the general left for the smoking room followed by his guests.

Where they to smoke tobacco and set a bad example our readers.

Yes, and a good thing too it was alien funny whacky stuff, so they never heard the mauling the pets gave the guard in a corridor.

It was time to escape.

"That is my signal," Dorothy and ran to the SOUND OF THE GUNS, in this case, a cat hissing and shredding and a dog hanging onto moons.

"Where my friend goes so do I?" Susanna needing Dorothy to handle that cat.

"Where my baby Doll goes so do I," Mcsweeny. *Oh yeh, what happened to,* "She is no longer my Baby Doll?" He knew the girls did succeed and leave him out of any rewards.

HAD IT NOT OCCURRED TO ANY OF THEM THAT THERE WAS NO REWARD. BEAG
WAS KNOWN TO HUMAN COMMAND.
EVEN THE HIGHWAY PATROL WERE LEAVING THEM.
WAKE UP FOOLS AND SNEAK AWAY HOME.

"Dorothy, I knew you did come," Beag having his hope fulfilled.
"Meow," Freckles throwing away what clung to a claw, it was a guard, an alien
who

when landing did sneak away much educated about

earth cats. A wise alien never having to clean a cat litter tray. Are there alien cats out there in space, yes, big ones that want to eat us, honest, I dreamed it.

"Woof," Jack and dropped the alien guard he had been shaking so the shaking alien sneaked away knowing he did never buy a dog from any planet.

Wise alien, never having to go walkies in the rain and scoop up dumps in bags. Are there alien dogs in space, yes, big ones that want to eat us, honest, I dreamed it.

"We will help you, come on then let us run to an exit," Mo at last with an idea but as he grabbed Beag, the little alien electrocuted him, just enough to let Mo know Beag belonged to LEG, not him.

"Jesus," Mo shaking being led behind the girls by Curly Jo and Larry.

"I have time to pick up this fallen alien weapon," McSweeny who did not have time as scanning cameras had detailed all and alarms were sounding in guards rooms.

And three undocumented immigrants hurried past him slapping each other so McSweeny relaxed thinking it was The Stooges.
It was those cousins trying to exterminate one another as the cousins knew they were no longer
        cousins but competitors, enemies.

They did tell cousin mothers cousins they immigrated to

Antarctica to study penguins. *Do you think the mothers did believe these boys?* And McSweeny, a film director chopped him on the run.

"Ha So hop," on the neck.

Why, a film director like an elephant never forgets
so always pays back.

Then drums beating, trumpets blaring, mythological sirens in mobile water tanks singing so
you did come to them to ogle as you were **Sons Of Adam and BE CAPTURED again.**

And in other tanks, the heads of Medusa, cloned, to turn you into STONE.

These were alien secret weapons whose price was being negotiated by a golfer to be the only Earth Leader

The question is, would the golfer allow our passengers to go home having met Beag and dined at the long table?

Who did believe them?

"I saw Nessie swim by the Statue of Liberty today."

"A Big Foot smashed my 4x4 with a rock, so it is a pile of rust."

"I am a victim of an alien abduction."

YEH and we listeners to this tale are all racing car drivers. Who did believe them?

And Mirror flew past McSweeny who tottered after the group and was slapped as mirror knew his type.

And McSweeny heard alien gibberish, sweet female choir singing and snakes hissing getting nearby.

Do not turn round McSweeny, those are Medusa's that will turn you to stone.

And he listened and did not turn round thus eliminating GORE from this tale for children.

If you want gore then to answer this, if you were the golfer and looking at the passengers would you trust any to keep quiet?

Would you allow them all to vanish to Dog Planet up amongst the stars where 'Simba's' and 'Mulan's' ancestors looked down upon you?

Or just vaporise them with the new weapons the alien general was selling you.

Yes, vaporise so no mess, sorry no gore.

CHAPTER 12 THE GREAT ESCAPE

Yes, a handy spare junior sized flying saucer for alien juniors to fly about Earth learning to fly, to abduct humans and not stay long enough for human papers to print, "ALIENS EXIST, THEY LANDED ON THE 'HOLLYSWOOD' SIGN. FEAR NOT THEY ARE TINY."

But was a mistake, they were juniors, squirts, shrimps, just wait till the parents arrived.

And **Lo and Behold** there was one of these junior craft parked in a corridor our passengers were thumping down secretly.

"THIS WAY OUT," *a handy sign next to the craft.*

And before anyone could say anything Susanna was in the drivers seat.

That woman driver again.

"I remember what this button is for," and went to press it.

And a robot nursery nurse appeared and pulled a Stooge

upside down to change his diaper.

"Beag do something?" Dorothy not wanting to see any more the more.

And the others huddled in a corner fearful they were next.

The Stooges being poor actors never bought new shorts, so we do not want to see what they have on.

Perhaps being so poor they bought no shorts as the price of shorts was coffee and doughnuts at Diego's, awe.

"Mother will be proud of me for changing my 'Y' fronts daily," Phillipo lying as he was the VILLAIN and all the excitement and lack of mobile latrines running across fields avoiding rubber rattlers and now rubber Gia Monsters, well, enough said.

"I always knew he was a stinker," Ronaldo being nasty and could he talk.

"I am a film director and carry disposable Y-Fronts in my back pocket next to my handy mobile phone that I use behind furniture to tell my film crew to bring in aliens into my Napoleonic film and it will be a Block Buster, YES, Napoleon abducted by aliens and replaced by a hybrid and why he lost Waterloo.

The French will love it as explains the defeat.

The English will hate it as takes away the GLORY of victory.

Away you go back to your make belief world of film props mister. Besides, he must have the last word, "When behind the furniture I not only use my mobile but change my 'Y' Fronts, so mummy did be proud of me.

No wonder this lot were seated amongst themselves at the dinning long table, they smelt BAD of unwashed unmentionables. Cur what a stink, even the alien flies buzzed away. Yes, alien flies that were starters as every now and again a tongue did dart out and swallow one.

They were aliens. They did eat earth dry of insect life and that did be the end of our pollinators.

"Dorothy will never look at me, sniff, cur, sniff, I am going to faint," Diego truthfully and did again so was blest as did not hear Suassuna shout, "Ignition keys," and turned them so the junior flying saucer blasted off, taking the exit door with it into an atmosphere.

An exit door made of plywood just for these occasions.

Aliens thought ahead.

The sudden thrust threw Freckles into the air.

What goes up must come down.

On the film director changing a disposable Y-Front.

"Sickening," the consensus of the others, even Susanna had to peek as she was a healthy girl who liked to look at male knobbly hairy knees that made her thank Jesus for the opposite.

"How could they walk about town with knees like those?" Susanna asked.

And Jack being a dog do what dogs do, grab the trousers going up and pulled.

"Jesus Christ," the film director and that is what a lot of people gasped.

A prayer an utterance of DISBELIEF.

Luckily, Jack pulled him into an open door which shut upon him.

Remember what goes up comes down went with him.

"Jesus Christ," was heard through the closed door.

What was it made off, yes, plywood.

He can stay in there as a minor character and unlucky to be in this exciting tale.

"Wee," Susanna "weeing," as the flying saucer zoomed away at 5000 mph.

Eyeballs swelled from Halloween Props.

Hair went straight up.

Teeth showed from gaping mouths.

"Titter," Susanna taking her hands of the steering wheel to pull down her skirt that inertia had pulled up.

And Dorothy felt like a poor pinned butterfly on the ceiling wall with her skirt blown up.

Her mind full of martial art moves as what goes up comes down for below her Diego holding onto a screwed down chair.

She could see by his bulging eye bawls he was ogling.

Never ogle at a woman uninvited, I hope your funeral expenses are paid up Diego, but knowing him, nope, just like the rest of us, the bill did go to the nearest relatives, his cousins who loved him dearly.

Horrid sounds of a mentally disturbed cat was heard behind a plywood door and a human begging "JESUS," he did attend church from now on IF "Jesus did kindly remove the cat," and whispered, "throw it out into space."

The film director had not read the gospels where Jesus gives the bullied cat to a village woman to look after AND CURSED THE BULLIES.

Like Him.

Why did Dorothy not ask Beag for help?

Her mouth was gaping, and her tongue was pressed against a cheek that is why, gravity.

As for Beag he was in a lotus position countering effects of sudden gravity and inertia change.

Mirror flew beside him fanning.

"I wonder what this lever is for. I know a handbrake?" Susana and pulled it back.

Yes, it was a brake and what goes up comes down.

Dorothy landed on Diego and bounced off, so he was a lucky man.

"No, I am not, the woman of my dreams was with me," gasp puff pant, "and now she is gone again, *rubbish,*" Diego.

A heavy duty capsule encased Susanna enjoying this driving lesson.

"20,000 m.p.h. awesome girls and boys," her proving the point.

There was no sounds of agreement from the passengers

pressed against walls, ceilings, and floor.

Even Freckles and Jack fell silent to the relief of the film director.

Did any protective capsules enclose the others, no but it did where they would have been sitting in chairs provided.

It was their own fault they decided to stand.

Alien insurance would not cover them.

"Hey, we are heading for the Moon, look guys the International Space Station, wave to them," Susanna waving and those aboard the station were aghast.

And Freckles went to a window and put on the saddest eyes of 'Puss and Boots,' and N.A.S.A. saw and hid the photos.

Even with the photos taken, NASA did say it was not a U.F.O. but a blown-up party prop of 'Taylor Swift' having escaped a party.

Yeh, we all know N.A.S.A., even if Beag got to them, they did send him back to Disney.

And Sussman full of mischief exposed her woolly thermal vest.

It did be concluded not all aliens were anatomically formless without male or female appendages or cats, they looked like a 'BABY DOLL,' *well done Susanna.*

And they passed the Station and went to the Dark Side of the Moon.

"What dark side?" Susanna asked her passengers.

Still silence.

"There is a big city down there and it is not flying the U.S.A. flag," Susana did not need spectacles, maybe the others after their eye-popping experience laser eye surgery.

"How do you land this tub?" Susanna and her passengers could still hear and went into a frenzied panic screaming silent, "NO," for they feared a crash landing.

And feared as all knew they did permanently visit a hot place down below.

Dorothy knew without her who did feed Freckles and Jack?

The film director was too young to die, he still had to make his greatest film yet, 'Tarzan Meets Dorothy,' of course with the pets as animals always steal the box office.

McSweeny wanted to get his new alien gun and blast the driver, Susanna but fortunately he was pressed against a wall.

The Stooges wanted out of this tale but could not so cried.

Phillipo knew things must be bad when they cry, so cried too.

And Ronaldo wanted to pray for forgiveness, rubbish, he wanted to kick Susanna out of the drivers seat and drive himself.

Diego wanted his greasy eatery back and forget this messy adventure, there were other Dorothy's wanting to eat his raw burgers so he could visit in hospital with flowers and chocolates and become friends.

So, none had confidence in Susanna's flying abilities.

Do you blame them?

She was a woman learner driver.

Where is that Beag, oh there he is.

"LEG," typically Beag close to Dorothy wondering why she and the others were strange positions.

"DO SOMETHING BEAG," it was mirror not wanting to become a thousand shreds of silver.

So slowly as these scenes take time for the atmosphere to build up, Beag saw Sussans and the moons surface going away.

Susanna had not figured out how to stop, never mind landing.

And Beag used his mind and the ship slowed down.

Thudding sounds were heard as passengers dropped like flies.

A plywood door flew open and a film director in shredded clothes rolled out.

Somehow, he rolled to Susanna and tried to gnaw her ankles.

He was angry.

And The Stooges stopped crying and instead of straggling Susanna kissed her back, shoulders, and elbows ingratitude the ship has stopped peacefully.

Perhaps when they realised Beag had stopped the ship, the disgusting slurping kissing sounds did turn to anger, but the tale needs a romantic scene, and this is it. A violent scene to follow as Susanna beat the PLUMS out of them for smooching her back, shoulders, and straps, yes, the boys were Sons of Adams.

And McSweeny was too ill to WHAT? McSweeny, do you go about beating Baby Dolls? Are you one of them types? Of course not, he just wanted to give Susanna his alien gun he loved if she promised to stop driving.

But Phillipo was a villainous rotter who was whispering

soft nothings into Susanna's ears, "You did make a great getaway driver, come with me, and rob banks as the Highway Patrol Officers did never catch us at the speed this baby runs at.

And Susanna did like the saucer being referred to as a BABY, in the female so swivelled the chair she sat in about.

Oh, dear did she elbow Phillipo in the Adams apple? Did her fingers make middle fingers in his eyes, was that her knees going places?

She just did not like Phillipo, *he was a villain.*

"I prefer Diego rather than you," Susanna and Diego heard.

Foolish girl.

Here he comes.

"Hello handsome," it was Dorothy, was she serious?

"AT last," Diego and sighed and from a handy back pocket produced a small book and out of it a pressed flower.

That touched Dorothy's soul but not enough and with a click Beag was beside her, and she pointed at Diego and flicked a finger backwards.

So, Dorothy was not serious in her words after all.

"Thud," behind her, "I will keep this," catching a pressed flower wafting down.

Then U.F.O.s surrounded their ship.

Beag waved to them nervously.

"What is the matter Beag?! Dorothy asked.

Beag sucked his thumb in silence.

"They are greys," Mirror spoke for Beag in a voice that filled

the cabin with chirping songbird songs and coloured ribbons flew out of the mirror and the smell of sweet peas smelt.

"GREYS?" McSweeny going for his gun, but he had given it away. He now did the right thing he went behind Phillipo; villains were expendable not good guys like him. The GREYS could take Phillipo first away to Planet ABC and put him in a zoo fed doughnuts 24/7 as aliens knew what humans ate, they watched 'Homer Simpson.'

Did they know about Diabetes? What did alien zoological classes teach, nothing.

"GREYS?" Phillipo having read pulp fiction dime comics, but McSweeny was standing on his feet so explains the funny faces. Phillipo hoped the GREYS did think his expressions of pain were a sign of disease and leave him alone. And not give him experimental enemas, yes, the comics the GREYS read were explicit.

"GREYS?" The Stooges remembering the parts they got playing GREYS in the film, 'Greys from Planet ABC invaded Las Vegas 1941," and were shot up, beat up but fed burgers, fries and coke before the film set moved on, without them or paying them or Diego so took a month to wash and dry Diego's greasy dishes with spit and polish as Diego was a miser to clear the bill.

"I made that B Class film and food was their pay," the film director remembering everything bad about GREYS. They ate you.

"I watch 'Blaze T.V. and know aliens come in funny colours. Beware of rainbow-coloured ones *unless you are*," and Diego

thought he was funny but not McSweeny who slapped, kicked, and head-butted Diego as McSweeny saw a chance to show of his manliness.

"I got to get out of here, I know GREYS abduct you to take parts away from you so am keeping my parts, "Ronaldo and tried opening the walls, but there was no handles so ended up sobbing imaging himself on a dissecting table in an anatomy class watched by millions of GREY students via cable.

"Let them come," Dorothy twirling McSween's alien gun. She knew GREYS appeared at your bedside wakening you.

What where they doing at your bedside? Watching you. They were perverts and Dorothy knew what to do with perverts, "Freckles, Jack," she called.

"GREYS?" Susanna and from a hidden pocket took foundation and lipstick. Aliens had a film industry and here was her chance to be a star as all the other actors did be GREY.

And Mirror hid down Beag's trousers, so he giggled and was no help at all, the useless twerp of a cute alien.

"Follow us," the voice of a GREY over the intercom.

"They know English?" McSweeny.

Susanna's hopes went sky high; she knew learning languages was not her best asset.

"From all the abductees they dissected," Ronaldo.

And Susanna answered by pushing the gas lever forward.

"Wee," Susanna.

"Jesus Christ," "I have marked by shorts," "I hate the woman," "My false teeth left me," "I think my arm broke," "She is my getaway driver," "Where is my gun, it can handle this," "She can replace all my stunt folk." "Beag stop giggling, do something," "Hiss," "Woof," "Tra La Le Beag yes do something, by the way you need a wash." Yes, Beag had the mentality of a year one kid just going into High School and the body of a little man so smelt like a boy just finding how his body works.

The year one meant he smelt of BOY and skid marks, had a folded down page of a page from a naughty publication and smeared hair gel on his hair and wiped it off on his seat, and at the same time played with little cars, plastic soldiers, and LEGO and when you were not looking, 'Barbie.'

Beag had strange ideas about LEG.

Was dangerous, it worshipped LEG, and had Beag realised LEG was part of Dorothy?

We the readers and storyteller know Beag is an alien, would he while she slept steal LEG wearing a GREY mask, so they did be blamed.

Just remember, aliens ate humans as I like you read science fiction dime novels, watch paranormal shows, and allow my imagination to tell me the truth.

They eat our kids, take our woman in abductions, which might be all right as she nagged nonstop, put on rubber human skins, and take our jobs.

We know this is true as we watched 'Men in Black,' films one and two and 'Martians like Earth Girls.'

He needed to be sent to Area 51, they knew what to do with aliens, they gave them to 'Men in Black.'

And at WARP SPEED the craft did not take long to reach Planet ABC and in front of them they could see floating cities above polluted oceans. Homes to billions of GREYS.

Alien diapers flattened against the craft's screen.

Susanna freaked at the contents.

Yes, Greys wanting Earth to build floating cities and have us as diaper disposal units.

I look at the photos N.A.S.A. rejects taken on Mars showing tracks made by a heavy vehicle. A waste disposal vehicle driven by abductees.

I am always right.

Aliens are on the moon, living in burrows so we do not see them. Just like on Earth they live in undersea cities encouraging us to go to war amongst ourselves, and when we are decimated, conquer us.

How do I know this, I can read teacups and coffee dregs. All you must do is pull the string on your 'Buzz Light Year Doll,' and look at the stars and tremble with fear.

Aliens eat humans.
They steal our kids to bring up as aliens.
They make hybrids of alien abductees.

They are here.

CHAPTER 13 GREYS

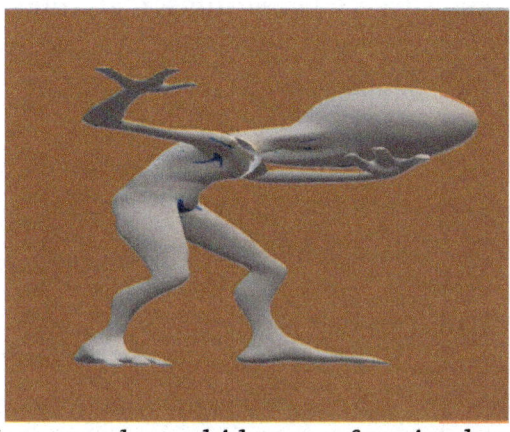

A Grey, naked as usual, yes hide your face in shame "You naked thingmabob."

And way back in Space Time, an alien general was not happy. An ASPIRER had been in touch with his emperor telling everything from the brand of toothpaste used, see these aliens had teeth hidden where the mouth should be, teeth for eating humans, so does the general snore.

And the emperor ripped up the general's paycheck, a bad omen to he general, he also sent the aspirer to help Beag.
Was this alien emperor thinking?
Yes, but he was the emperor.

Aspirers should be rewarded with dangerous one-way missions.
And just like that the aspirer appeared next to Beag, looked at the screen and flipped.
"I am too young to die," in perfect Kings English with marbles.

And blame Susanna who was clutching Dorothy's legs, "I am just a girl, I never asked for this life, I was dealt bad cards as a baby, I do not want to see anything like that again, I do not want babies, Dorothy are you listening?"

Anyone looking at the viewing screen did know they were about to crash into a floating tower block were aliens stopped lounging on the garden roof to seek shelter from the fast-approaching craft.

And the aspirer had forgotten rays came forth and held the craft still, yes once again passengers thudded places.

"Mo, who is driving?" Larry hoping.

"Meow," a reply from a smart cat at the controls. Yes, a smart cat that had watched Susanna drive and knew all you did was pull this lever AND PRESS THE GREEN BUTTON. Just as well the craft was held by gravity rays and was now being gently put down on a floating Central Park.

And the passengers looked at Freckles admiringly.

Once back home they did hire the cat to Disney to remake 'That Darn Cat.'

They knew this was a smart cat.

They knew if the cat could land a spaceship, it could drive them home nights out, and fill up emergency.

Anyway, we have the problem of the aspirer aboard ship now. Sent into exile as a helper to Beag. But his heresy tales had done the job, the general was in deep never mind.

And in the wings, a favourite first cousin of the emperor waiting to be THE NEW GENERAL and keep power in the family. He was a silent aspirer, just waiting to slip that cat behind the controls of the imperial ship.

Aspirers every where.

And the craft doors opened and there stood a giant handsome human, and as smaller greys ushered the passengers out, it was seen this humanoid had black wings.

Black wings the opposite of white wings.

Trouble.

He was some sort of angel.

Did this mean the greys were naughty folk, yes it does.

"I am Nephilim 265, your guide here," but never said where here was. And why a Nephilim as a guide, well, this was a city of GREYS, those aliens that are blamed for abductions and never mind.

All I know aliens eat your children, steal your nagging wives, and in-laws, take your jobs and identity and leave you to ride the trains as a hobo.

Am I right reader.

And Susanna let go off Dorothy. Some girls just never learn, in fact some folks never learn. She was overcome by Nephilim's

256 beauty. It radiated from him, it glowed from his arm pits, his teeth blinded you with silver light, his bum seeped creaking light and his enormous cod piece threatened to burst light.

And McSweeney huffed and puffed his chest up, but he was nowhere compatible to Nephilim 256 whose hairless chest shone of olive oil.

Well, what do you know, he had genuine feeling for Susanna or something else, remember this is McSweeney.

And as Susanna played with Nephilim's real 'Austin Power' chest that had droplets of olive oil trapped amongst it. Susanna just flicked them behind her. McSweeney shed an olive oil tear.

"Baby Doll," he whispered heartbroken, and she heard and looked back at him. For an instant she was deciding, him or this alien hulk.

What would 'Baby Doll' decide?

What would you reader decide?

Especially if you are a girl from next door, I know, take the oily hulk, and collect the olive oil droplets to cook with as mummy said, "Never waste what money bought sweetie."

"Susanna," it was Beag who knew she was making a mistake, she should be after him, no, that is a mental slip reader, Beag was concerned. He had been eve dropping into everyone's thoughts, as an alien he can do that, *as well as eat you.*

And Freckles and Jack came over and sat looking up into Susiana's eyes.

She could only make one decision reader.

Choose them to keep the pet food coming.

1] She picked up Freckles and threw the cat on Nephilim 256 as she remembered well her time with men like him.

2] She picked up Jack and thrust him a place where dogs like to sniff and embarrass you on Nephilim 256 and bit and clung on.

3] Having two hands and opposing thumbs Susanna managed both 1 and 2 together.

4] I remember my Sunday school lessons and know who you are big boy.

And The Stooges ran past Nephilim 256 and accidently pushed him over plus giving out a few slaps.

Down into the floating city The Stooges went straight to a greasy Grey alien eatery parked on the grass where it looked like human kids played tag, Frisby, hide and sneak and scrabble.

And the Mo asked for three Margheritas with Nanco French Fries without asking if they spoke English, or accepted I.O.U.'s.

That explains why all the kids gathered about him.

"We watch Earth films, we recognise you, you are the funny men who like being slapped," a cute little girl in pigtails smiling.

Then just like that she levitated and slapped the daylights out of The Stooges.

Then the pizzas arrived, about a hundred, and the children opened their mouths exposing shark teeth.

Mo stood back onto Curley Joe who toppled back onto Larry who just fell backwards.

Just like that with lots od munching sounds the pizzas were all gone.

"He is paying," Mo shoving Curly Joes forward who handed over a ten-cent coin.

HYBRID, COMEDY SCIENCE FICTION

Silence.

Then the eatery alien laughed loudly and waved over a passing disc with an obvious law enforcement officer riding it.

Obvious as the disc had that alien emperor's face on the sides, and a foghorn and blue light cluttered the disc.

The Grey wore a white helmet with a badge on it and dark glasses were present, as well as the array of heavy weapons hanging from a belt.

"They did not pay," the proprietor shouted.

"Beag do something please," Dorothy.

"They did not pay," Beag answered.

"I am Nephilim 256 and will pay," and looked at the girls. "Come," he said to Susanna raising his eyebrows often.

"Remember I went with this angel to save The Stooges," Susanna posing in a pose of sadness.

A yellow cab drew up.

Nephilim 256 opened the door for her to enter.

Beag, we need her to fly this craft back to Earth, please do something," Dorothy pleaded.

"Mirror let us go," Beag who levitated after the yellow cab that flew up to join hundreds of yellow cabs.

"Mirror will bring her back, and Beag," mirror and followed Beag.

"This is my time to take command of the craft and make these humans my crew," the aspirer.

"You were saying?" McSweeney picking him up flexing biceps and used the aspirer as a towel to wipe himself down.

And Nephilim 256 did not pay, he was a fallen angel, of the race that sired giants with Earth women.

And The Three Stooges spent time autographing.

"We watch Earth films, Jaws, Alamo, Midway, Taxi Driver and best of them all, The Stooges," the cute little girl with pig tails and teeth like a shark.

The parents of these darlings came over and paid and ordered pizza for The Stooges.

Just like Earth, no pay but fed.

And McSweeney sat in the craft's drivers seat sobbing.

"My Baby Doll," he moaned and used the aspirer to wipe away his tears and clean wax from the ears.

That is how small the aspirer was.

A titch.

Then threw the soaked alien aside.

"You are an alien, get my get away driver Susanna back and join my gang, it is called 'The Good, The Bad, The Ugly and Phillipo," what about it?" Phillipo knowing one alien was as good as another.

Was he right reader, did the aspirer have Beag's powers?

He had not worshipped LEG yet.

He spoke intelligently with the reasoning of an adult, whereas Beag spoke like a child.

He did not have a mirror to fix his mistakes.

He wanted power, if not back home, then where on earth and his new subjects were in front of him, they just needed bribed.

What could he bribe them with.

Coins with his emperor's face on them and be accused of counterfeiting with monopoly money.

And his reflection stared back at him, it was the answer. The reflection, no, him, he could promise them to turn himself in and give them the alien reward if they obeyed him in everything.

Do you mean everything?

Yes, when he used the squares in the latrine you were there. I hear in Japan a robot hand appears and does that, all right enough plumbing talk.

He was the bribe, but was he smart enough to realise that.

NO, he was an alien, able to fly across the stars but unable to conquer Planet Earth, so that is why he is not smart enough to out smart our passengers how do I know, because any fool knows when you turn yourself in for the reward on yourself you go STRAIGHT TO GAOL from the property you are resting on, and you are forgotten about, except for Johnny Cash.

'The gifts They Gave,' and the aspirer gave none.

And legs apart stood in the aspirers way.

A cute cat and a panting dog were under the legs.

"I was top pf my social interaction classes with humans and know their pets are harmless and see why Beag," and began to mumble as he focused on those legs as he got nearer to the ship's controls.

What should he have been focusing on?

To late, Freckles raked him, and Jack snapped him where a place was hidden.

He could have screamed, but that would have proven humans are a superior species, and anyway he was in deep shock so could not.

Yes, we are the dominant species.

Just look at how we exterminate our pollinators.

Our oceans.

Block our drains with non flushable diapers.

And eat anything with a good sauce, like the aspirer and aboard ship Wayne whispered, "Tastes like pork, he is not human so can serve him up in a hot chocolate souffle and he can be the marshmallow," Wayne not liking the aspirer as not been bribed by him yet.

See, I am proven correct, we are smarter than the aliens.

Anyone reading this article did have bribed the aspirer for power, so we are smarter or why is it always a human the Captain of The Enterprise in Star Trek, Kirk, Lorca, Georgiou, and many others we never remember.

And Dorothy used a leg to flick him away and he landed in a latrine and the door shut and the roll of paper heard.

Then screaming.

The pets were absent.

*

Susanna's adventure.

Remember she was the girl from next door, yes her that when the parents were out you played 'Scramble' with, so had to leave town in a hurry.

Susanna knew she was not paying the taxi as she cuddled into that olive oily smooth chest, and frisked pockets.

Nephilim 256 was impressed she carried money, it meant she could pay for the takeaway meal he was about to order from his commode.

And what a commode, it had Athenian Colonnades, fairy Hounds of Celtic bra cups Lore waited to greet him at the entrance of his home.

Susanna dug deep into her elastics and produced Jerky Chews which she used to make friends with these hounds.

Nephilim 256 was more impressed.

Inside was a maze of flowering Plants whose perfumes were meant to swoon Susanna making her defenceless.

From her bra cups she pulled out a Covid 19 face mask.

And sprayed on her own perfume.

Nephilim 256 was impressed.

So impressed his heat rate increased.

He was a Horney Nephilim on the make.

And swooped up Susanna who titter and moaned putting the act on.

Then "Kiss me Baby Doll," Nephilim 256.

She had heard this line many times.

His drooling kisses were soaking her attire, almost drowning the girl.

It was when his hands went a roaming Susanna remembered what she had said to her fellow passengers, "I will be back," soon not in nine months time ready to give birth.

Nephilim 256 was taken out by Susanna by a knee, finger in the eye pokes, and the use of what every good girl from next door carries on her, pepper spray.

Screaming holding his eyes Nephilim 256 ran into a Corinthian Colonnade, this male liked his colonnades, so knocked him self out.

"This is a big house, it has all we need to escape this planet and get back to Plnet Earth," Susanna and here shows us,

1] See was remembering her fellow passengers, she was not leaving them behind, anyway they did cram into the junior spaceship, so she was stuck with them.

2] So gave the Nephilim an extra dose of pepper spray as she figured tit did take her half an hour to frisk this place and explains why as she passed Nephilim 256 with a canvas bag full of 'SWAG' she sprayed more pepper spray onto his face.

We got to feel sorry for Nephilim 256, all he wanted was the girl next door, the bad Nephilim full of whatever drives a Nephilim, a high dose of testerone.

3] As she passed Nephilim 256, she pulled down a curtain rope and tied him up, then sprayed him good, hit the back of his head with one of her red shoes, then dug tastier jerky up and went outside.

4] The whistle she gave brought the Fairy Dogs, which was what the jerky was for, thus proving humans are smarter than aspiring aliens. And a yellow cab appeared hovering near her.

She got in, she threw out the alien taxi driver. She had no idea how to ask directions back to the junior ship, but she could remember the way back.

What a girl from next door.

*

"Hide," Mo's sensible command to the other two Stooges.

A yellow cab was lurching towards them at speed.

Where could they hide, where McSweeny pulled them out from, under the junior space craft, yes, a sensible place to hide when the approaching yellow cab hit.

And Dorothy looked out the cockpit screen and did not

hide, she saw Susanna at the controls of the yellow cab, a woman was driving, there was nothing to fear.

And behind her a film director was on his knees praying holding onto her new skirt so tightly he shredded it. That was his excuse. Dorothy knew better, she flicked him away with a leg so three splats were heard behind. Phillipo had been sneaking up with the heavily bandaged aspirer to overpower Dorothy and take command of this ship.

Outside Ronaldo stood behind Diego for protection when the yellow cab arrived and at an open window Susanna waved a handbrake to the fellow passengers, she was saying, "Where is the brake," but still Dorothy had confidence Susanna did safely land the cab.

And from nowhere a small alien dressed as a caped crusader standing on his mirror zoomed up to Susanna. The alien waved at Dorothy and blew her a kiss.

"Beag," Wyne waving back. Hey, wait a moment, to whom was Beag blowing the kiss.

And Dorothy blew a kiss back.

Something in Dorothy's mind told her, her little cute alien had graduated from primary school and was now in year one of High School. The word cute did be dropped from her vocabulary when addressing Beag, there was no reason in encouraging the boy to grow up quickly, let him enjoy his childhood.

And it was Beag using mental powers that landed the yellow cab outside the junior spaceship.

And Dorothy was proved correct, there was no reason to worry when a girl from next door was driving.

And Susanna dragging her bag of SWAG entered the other ship ready to fly them back to Planet Earth.

After hugs and praises a head count was done.

Diego and Ronaldo were missing.

Moans and pleads for help were heard coming from outside. Everyone just had to look and Beag tittered with embarrassment, proving he was still a cute little alien for he had landed the yellow cab upon these missing two.

Was it deliberately done?

He never liked them.

Was it attempted murder?

No, he was just hoping to leave them behind, like said, he did not like them, and in a child's mind that is good enough reason to jetson bag luggage.

And this time the passengers strapped themselves into the available seats aboard the junior spaceship that meant seat sharing.

"Get lost Diego," Dorothy flicking him away against Phillipo.

"No room here," The three Stooges slapping Ronaldo away.

"Definitely no way," McSweeny all tough 'Die Hard' detective when a film director tried sitting on his lap who then held onto Diego who held onto McSweeny's legs.

And McSweeney could not swat them off without releasing his seat belt so did the next best thing, he glared at them.

And Susanna did not do safety checks as did not have a flying licence or a make sure the passengers were using the seat belts.

She pressed that green button and without thinking used the joystick and foot pedals to fly the craft into the atmosphere and freedom.

See a cute little alien was enjoying puberty and wanted to enjoy it more so was using thought control over Susanna to fly this craft, and mirror was using thought control on him, see, Beag came last in all his classes, which meant flying lessons also.

Mirror did not want to be a thousand silver pieces.

And below "Baby Doll, I thought we had something good going," Nephilim 256 outside his house next to his Colonnades,

and because the Fairy Dogs had been spoiled by a woman's jerky, mauled him good. Why a woman had stuffed his pockets full of jerky.

Not to worry he no doubt had healing energies and the dogs did be given jerky treats from now one, see, something always good is there if you look.

CHAPTER 14   SAUCER COMMAND 4

Beag's Emperor

And The General had decided to back his human friend to

conquer Planet Earth. The idea being to instal his golfing friend as Emperor of The United Nations as The General had enough upstairs to realize the human leaders there did not accept him YET as Emperor Above Emperors, and when that time came, there did be a golfing accident.

A caddie did have a mental breakdown, suffering from

depression and make the golfer swallow twenty unwashed golf balls, then drive the electric golf buggy this way and that over the golfer till he was alone and then speed away in the electric golf buggy to freedom.

And because of The Men in Black, it never happened, but it was an original assassination idea from The General, see, aliens thought crocked, it would have worked on another alien, but the golfer was a human.

And The General remembered a film, 'Alien' and knew he

had to have that alien to win. Did he not remember that alien ate everyone, no, The General was an alien, he knew he would not be affected so played with the computer to find THAT ALIEN in space.

What a man.

And his emperor decided to visit, Planet Earth looked so nice in blues and greens, just like Planet Mars once did.

It happened thus:

The General was at his long table emersed in his wristwatch computer seeking TH|AT ALIEN eating eyeball gob suckers. Extra hot chilli-soaked alien eyeballs boiled hard needing sucked.

A pitcher of ice-cold water was present also.

"Hello," his emperor appearing out of a misty space time warp and was seen by the others at the dining table, so they stood at attention, all aspirers understand.

Except The General did not stand at attention as he was sucking an extra hot alien eyeball.

It was the second "Hello," that got the attention of The General who recognising the voice of his emperor sucked in and sucked in the alien eyeball extra chilli hot.

It was one of Wayne's culinary inventions, and the eyeballs came from, a fish tank that grew them.

No wonder Wayne was glad to vacate his kitchens because eyes were watching your every move, so unnerving.

The extra chilli was pure nastiness as Wayne remembered all The General's jokes about him being cooked as a main course.

"Wheeze," The General sucking the eyeball deeper down his airways.

Then he grabbed the purple muslin robes beside him and coughed up the eyeball extra chilli hot.

Muslin studded with fine beaten gold flakes.

Long strands of mucus clung to the alien eyeball and dribbled down to the gold painted sandals, dribbling between the toes.

Then The General grabbed the gem encrusted belt about the wobbly belly that came from overeating and pulled himself up and the belt and fine purple muslin down.

There were gasps of astonishment, their emperor had a weeny weenie on the tiny size.

Laughter filled the room.

The emperor's face went red with rage, so he tried to speak but spit went out instead.

That was lucky for The General as it gave him command to order his emperor arrested and jettisoned into space, if only he could stop laughing.

And the praetorian guard did not aid their emperor as were laughing too.

And unknown to them a junior spaceship was speeding their way on a collision course, but the mother ship here had a coxswain remember, he did steer the mother ship out of a collision course, if he could stop laughing.

And a human golfer burst into laughter and so did The Men in Black, these aliens were comical, humans had nothing to fear from aliens, the aliens were a bunch of clowns.

And that is when the cadie stuffed twenty unwashed golf balls down the golfer's mouth and took flight to safety in the caddie cart, a cart whose top speed was ten miles per hour.

Do you think he made it to Mexico?

"I want that alien to sit at my diner table tonight so while I eat roast ground hog in a Newman barbecue sauce, I can watch him eat twenty golf balls, unwashed of course.

"Yes Sir," The Men in Black and roared way in handy nearby golf buggies after the alien assassin at ten m.p.h.

*

"I am too young to die," Phillipo shouted seeing a collision, then remembered at the last moment Susanna landed so gently, so relaxed.

"Do you think The General will be glad to see us?" Ronaldo

knowing the answer.

"We better change course for earth," Diego.

"We have nothing to fear, a girl is at the helm and Beag is nearby," Dorothy wanting not to go to heaven early.

"I have my weapon Baby Doll," McSweeny and did not add "magnum," so was thought as a dirty young man.

"Mo do something," Curly Jo and Larry and pushed Mo onto Susanna. A silly thing to do when the driver was trying to remember where the anchor was.

The first The General knew trouble was at hand was when he saw Susanna's face cross the viewing screen.

She was holding levers and wires in her hands.

He was not amused.

"Wat is a human female driver doing at the controls of," and never finished as his emperor the only one not laughing jumped him.

That was a signal for all aspirers aboard ship to jump them both, some stab with fingers, some with erasers, others what they grabbed on the way over, smaller aliens with many limbs and used them as batons.

"I am not amused," the emperor standing with tentacles clinging to his head.

The fool, he had his back to The General who coshed him with one of those many limbed aliens in one hand, and the ships gear lever he had yanked up in the other hand, yes, that did the trick, the emperor sank to his knees and was covered in aspirers just like that.

Then there was turbulence as a junior ship hit them.
It happened thus:

"Hey kiddo, try this," Dorothy holding out a Kirby grip and Beag passed it on to Susanna. With this instrument of womanhood, she poked and twisted in a hole where something had been yanked out.

Sparks passed up her hand, so her hair became the branches on a tree.

"Beag do something," Dorothy pleaded and Beag did do anything for Leg.

He opened the exit door while the ship was slowing down to say, a hundred m.p.h.

The Stooges held each other tightly but did not hold onto anything else so they flew out the exit door because a villain we know had pressed the red release button on their seat belts.

"Three shares less," Phillipo straining to get in the seat.

"Bye cousin never liked you," Ronaldo flicking Phillipo's nose, so he jerked back and out the exit door.

"Yes, bye cousin," Diego and kicked him out and doing so meant he went too.

"Ah, a seat," the oily film director locking himself into the seat.

What of those that went out exit?

They would be dead, Boo Hoo, out of this tale.

A thunderclap was heard as something broke the speed of sound, what a din so alien and human clapped ears. Yes, ears came forth like the plagues of Egypt out of the sides of our green, black-eyed aliens.

Many alien ear drums popped so goo shut forth like clowns fired from a circus cannon.

Very messy.

It tended to stick to you and where it came from forming long sticky chains of GOO.

Worse it smelt of cat pee.

And The General was tied up in this GOO, thus unable to be 'Master and Commander in this Far Side of The Moon.'

"Hail the new Emperor Fig," someone hoping to be promoted by Emperor Fig so remains anonymous in case the old emperor covered in many limbed aliens proved an obstacle.

And who was Fig? Someone who was addicted to earth figs, so we know heaps about him from this.

And the face of Mrs. Frankenstein appeared across the viewing screen.

It was Susanna suffering from the electric shock.

And what broke the speed of sound appeared with Beag riding it in his cape defender out fit. Already it had opened at the seams showing far too much.

And that adolescent Beag enjoyed his growing up last moments as the junior spaceship was a hundred yards from the mother ship.

And Beg used his mental powers and stopped the collision so the junior ship gently nosed the mother ship.

"Three cheers for our Susanna," Mo and the passengers cheered and did not crowd about her to paw as she looked like Mrs Frankenstein.

"Here let me help you sister," Dorothy coming to whisk up Susanna's hair and tart up her face with extra long eye lashes and foundation and rouge.

"Baby Doll," McSweeny in love.

"She looks tarty," Phillipo being nasty and how did he know what tarts looked like?

Because he was a villain.

And Dorothy dressed Susanna in a black open skirt and nylons and pinned a French cap to her bundles of blonde hair.

And Diego knew he had to marry her.

Hey, thought he wanted to marry Dorothy, he still does, he was a bigamist.

And that aspirer aboard ship opened the exit door unaware of events on the mother ship, he thought he did leap out praising his emperor and claiming the capture of these trouble some humans.

He was a real oily character, far worse than the film director.

But as he finished his sentence Dorothy threw Freckles upon him.

The Emperor Fig stood with legs apart waiting for gifts.

The gift was Jack who jealous of the cat ran upon him.

Then McSweeny jumped out somersaulting blasting his magnums missing everything he aimed at as you ever try and fire magnums when somersaulting?

And the alien troops dressed as Roman Legionaries fled. They were aliens and usually won against humans when flying saucers, manning giant war robots, and spreading terror by abductions.

In this Science fiction tale, the humans win, or no one did be alive to tell the tale. The Stooges could tell but they did turn the tale into one of their episodes.

"Whir," the sound of a camera as the film director from his belt button.

"Hello Mummy," Phillipo blowing kisses at the camera lens.

There was no emperor, the aliens needed a leader to rally them.

"I volunteer to be emperor," Ronaldo seeking gain.

And a mirror went across his head shaving.

On the mirror stood Beag.

And a small figure ran to stand under him, "I will be emperor," Wayne.

And "Hail Emperor Beag," a shout and became a chant.

"My little alien has all grown up," Dorothy not realising the implications of what she just said.

And The General struggling to move in goo tried to apprehend Beag, but the troops sprayed him with a mist that became a net. "I wanted to be emperor," he whined.

"I am Emperor Fig," he whined also.

"But I am the real emperor," and as we are never told his name can ignore him.

Why are there no females for this elevated job because they have more sense.

*

The coronation was a sham, it happened thus:

They crowded back onto the mother ship and headed for Planet \earth.

"Look mummy a flying saucer," an earth kid.

"We are being invaded by Martians, here take this," a man on the sidewalk with a bigger magnum than McSweeny.

Police sirens blared.

"I am The Commander in Chief, kill them then ask what they want?"

Fighter jets took the air.

National Guardsmen drove here and there kin military green trucks waving at folk.

Women ran up to them at traffic lights and smooched these heroes. Many of these trucks drove away with giggling and the sound of elastics being twinged out the back of the trucks.

What was going on, these guys were alien killers so what where they up to in the back of the trucks. I know swamping their stamp collections.

Highway Patrol officers on motorcycles provided a noisy escort.

And where was this all going on, Holly Wood of course for the mother ship was not choosy where it wanted to land.

And who was steering the mother ship, a demonic woman with blond hair with a French black capon it.

A French tart.

"I will make you a film star if you land on the Holly Wood sign Susanna," an oily soft whisper and we can all guess who this is.

And way below an R.V., a camper, a fire truck, a 4x4 where being towed to the police pound.

And Susanna blinked as one of those extra long French tarty black eye lashed came lose and got in an eye.

"No," the film director repeated often but then brightened, squashing the evidence of their past crimes was a brilliant idea of Susanna's and then the earth folk did think it a hostile action and he could jump out and negotiate terms, on Global TELEVISION.

Had he forgotten he was one of these earth folks?

And the R.V. loo door opened and the R.V. owner came to stand outside.

"Where have you guys been, you mean I missed all the action sitting on the throne, no wonder my moons got cramp," the R.V. owner not amused and a motorcycle police officer seeing him come out and said, "One of them I have seen on television's must wanted and a $10,000 reward for their capture dead or alive." so yes, the R.V. owner was not amused.

And on the Holly Wood hill a flying disc with Beag on it with a mirror shading him from the sun.

Millions of aliens with fans and purple carpets ran out of the mother ship hailing "Emperor Beag."

"My cute little alien," Dorothy.

And Beag let power go to his brain if he had one for, he remembered LEG.

And just like that Dorothy was beside him on the small disc which meant she had to cling to Beag or fall off.

The crafty little cute alien.

More like the dirty little alien pervert who needs the vet.

"Who is that woman, she is straight out of 'Flash Gordon, I must own her," an earthly man with power.

"Hey, these aliens are handing out pizza and jam doughnuts, they are friendly, and ten-dollar bills," it just Takes one.

And "Hail the Emperor Beag," another.

"Of Earth," as the aliens handed out hundred-dollar bills.

"I must get down there and get my share," he who wanted Dorothy added to his collection.

See, some earth men with power are just like earth men without power.

And Susanna walked out.

"She is better to my liking," this man *but remember many adults are not like him*, it was just that Susanna like the Greek Mythological Siren oozed "I am a woman, come here Baby Boy."

And with a whisk Susanna tossed aside her French hair style and black cap and in a whirl of motion that was her spinning at 1000 m.p.h. all those tarty clothes went too.

"Cur," the humans.

"*" as aliens are thought senders.

And McSweeney shouted, "Baby Doll marry me," and as there was no reply added, "please," and still no reply as Susanna had been married twenty times already always falling to "PLEASE.

McSweeney you better do better, readers what can he do and say to win Susanna?

Give advice please

"Beag get off my leg and do something, please," Dorothy but not to worry MIRROR was female and helped while Beag having matured had grown six inches that meant, HE COULD REACH DOWN TO LEG WITHOUT BENDING.

I told you readers, this was no cute alien, were our Commander in Chief, oh yes, down there with the ordinary folk with a carrier bag collecting hundred-dollar bills.

"VISIT MARI LARGO," was on a sticker on the carrier bag.

"Hello Mister having fun?" We ask him.

"$," in his eyes greet nus.

The Planet earth is doomed.

And because the mother ship landed on a hilltop blocked a sewer outlet pipe, THAT MEANT IT HAD TO GO ELSE WERE.

Up your toilet bowel, we all experienced neighbours flushing away diapers, cat litter and never mind.

"What a stink," one of those earthlings with hundred-dollar bills stuffed down his 'Y' Fronts so even if one escaped, I did nor pick it up.

Do you agree reader?

So, the aliens went amongst the humans spreading diseases and love and thousand-dollar bills.

"Hey, book me a flight to Holly Wood," someone eating greasy burgers in a roadside café in New York, and a magnum was in a shoulder holster and a tin badge stuck on his belt.

We can forgive him as he was an under paid civil servant.

And only his spinning seat was there as he with a siren started driving to Holly Wood.

"My name is Kevin McSweeny and want away from the dark side of humanity," he explains stuck in rush hour traffic.

Anyway:

And Beag clothed Susanna as he remembered from classes what earth girls looked like in the 1950's.

McSweeny's heart was breaking, "I am sorry I call you baby Doll; I do not know what else to call you."

And she heard and softened a bit.

He did have to prove he was willing to be different from the OTHERS.

Change the diapers.

Get up at feeding times.

Take the dog out.

Clean dog mess yes.

Change cat litter.

Change the newspaper in the bird cage.

Have a shower.

Cook breakfast for the ten other kids.

Pay the news paper boy.

Take the ten other kids to education.

Go to work and when you come home, we will talk about extras, if you ARE UP TO IT, if not I have a girls bowling night, all right?

Susanna was learning.

Was she so mean.

And Beag, "Here is my Empress," and there was a pause.

YES?

He gritted his teeth that appeared from where teeth should be.

"LEG."

There was silence

"Yeh a leg like that we can worship and obey," a human ogler.

"Yeh, looks better than our grisly old leaders," another.

And before Dorothy noticed humans crowded about the disc demanding LEG walk amongst them so they could touch, stroke, and throw flowers upon LEG.

They had another thing coming, Beag was a selfish cute little alien who was having nothing of it.

"Exterminate them," he said.

"What did you say Beag?" Dorothy.

"Yeh, what said the emperor say?" A human ogler.

"IT said exterminate them," a reply from a bus driver.

"You mean those Men in Black in sunglasses?" A girl scout so no one panicked.

"Awesome," and "Ouch," and "Owe," the human folk watching Dorothy . Beat the daylights out of Beag's moons.

Is this the end of Dorothy, we all know from films what

aliens do when a human does that, pull a laser, and exterminate the human; but this was The Emperess Dorothy, a human with LEGS and mirror dared anyone not to interfere so not an alien dressed as a Roman Legionary did.

"Hail Empress Dorothy," they hailed instead.

See Dorothy had pulled up and back her pleats so Beag could fit over a leg.

"LEG," Beag just before the first spank.

"Lucky cute little alien," a human ice cream vendor.

"Owe," aliens agreeing to wish they were over that leg.

All created Sons of Adams, readers of tabloid page three.

So, what was the point of having an expensive guard to protect you, there was no point, just a waste of cash that could have been better spent buying meals for poor kids in holidays.

And a golfer drove up in a convoy of a hundred golf buggies.

There was a fanfare.

Chorus girls and cheer leaders did their stuff circling the convoy.

"More Legs," Beag so his moons were beaten the colour of blue cheese and Dorothy began to pant and wheeze.

Oh, Dorothy that cute little alien is enjoying this.

And with that Dorohty flicked Beag asway.

"Epee yucky," she gasped in horror.

And Beag levitated with a sly look on his face.

He was a kid in puberty. Did Dorothy have both her stockings and was one missing.

Hey, look her bra was missing.

Was her elastics.

Beag was a kid in puberty suffering growing pains.

"Epee Yucky," Dorothy.

Then this Mannie under a red cap waving a golf club approached as the girl dancers parted for him to come to Beag.

"Are you Earth's Leader?" Beag asked the golfer now walking up to him.

"Not yet, I had a deal with The General to take over this world and with your help I can do it," this golfer not caring if he was heard and his remarks broadcast.

Now Beag remembered him and his General.

And Beag panicked as The General was like a headmaster with a cane, so he did not even apologise for vaporising this human Mannie.

"Beag what have you done?" Dorothy.

There was a little boy tittering.

"We have no leader, hey wait a moment the golfer was not our leader, yet" a Man in Black thus preventing WAR.

"Take us to the United Nations," it was Dorothy as Beag remember came last in his lessons so was thick as toast regarding earth politics.

Silence.

Then the cheer leaders and chorus girls danced into the mother ship and the convoy of Men in black.

The exhaust fumes must have been terrible and that explains aliens coughing running about with oxygen masks.

And all the earth generals and human oglers also.

Several food sellers too in case the aliens ate funny stuff.

They were off to The United Nations singing '9 to 5,' and garden dwarves were seen with shovels and picks singing, 'Hi Ho Off to Work We Go.'

"Do we not have a Mug Shot of her somewhere?" The real Commander in Chief waiting for Empress Dorothy in New York.

His right-hand fingers drumming a red button that did send warheads to vaporise these aliens landing in an election year.

But it was LEGS that stopped him starting a 'War of The Worlds' as he was transfixed, wondering if the wife still had legs like Dorothy. Well readers, we know what to call this Son Of Adam, "PERVERT."

"Sir, she is a commoner and done good for herself," a marine at attention and the Commander in Chief knew she was right. Without billions of dollars in backing this Dorothy was about to become Planet Earth's Leader.

This Dorothy was not even in his political party.

That was against ethics.

"She is an American citizen Sir," the female marine reading her bosses thoughts.

Females always stick together.

"This Dorothy does have nice legs though, nicer than yours sergeant," The Boss just promoting the female marine private.

Men, same everywhere, he should have his mind on meeting Emperor Beag and his earth empress.

Why at this moment staff were digging up information on Dorothy.

There was not much to tell, she was a beach bum. One of

those that smoked funny tobacco while sitting next to a log fire eating hot dogs and marshmallows.

Did Boss hear what was being said about Dorothy?

Of course, he just had his mind on her legs.

CHAPTER 15
LOOSE ENDS

The new confident Susanna

And Phillipo one for seeking 'El Doral do' sneaked into the mother ship.

"What is our thieving cousin doing?" Ronaldo who was a thieving cousin too.

"Claiming the alien reward as his own," Diego not content to leave things alone.

And the reason why Phillipo was sneaking away became apparent when motorcycle Highway patrol police officers surrounded these two.

"Look, he is escaping onto the mother ship, quick stop him before he gets away," Ronaldo a quick thinker and as the police officers looked, he was gone.

Where did he go?

It is a secret.

And Diego being slower in the mind than his cousin stood there gaping wondering why he was alone.

"You are under arrest son," and Diego felt cold handcuffs.

Do not feel sorry for him, as a police van awaited him and the R.V. owner was in it, so Diego did not be lonely but perhaps be murdered there as he explained to his fellow passenger how to fry greasy burgers and sell them.

And Beag and Dorothy entered the mother ship.

Now where was the Stooges?

They were pet minders as had managed to stuff Freckles into a cat basket AND muzzle Jack so explains why these brave men were covered in band aid and using crutches.

And as Dorothy stood next to the coxswain Beag had his mind on other stuff, he was an emperor with underlings who trimmed his nose hairs when they showed, painted faces on his phalanges, powder puffed his arm pits, flossed his teeth, and no, he was left to use the loo paper himself.

And Beag being in puberty made sure girl aliens pampered him, yes, do not believe tales on television aliens have no sexual thingmabobs.

They do or why make that film, 'Earth Girls are Easy.'

The film producer was a survivor of an alien abduction and knows.

These aliens are Horney little green monkeys so beware.

And Beag dreamed of his empress and building an arena full of exotic galactic fearsome creatures to throw those he did not like too.

He was an emperor and becoming a tyrant.

Was there no one to safe Planet Earth?

His empress who was not having any of this hanky panty or his floating mirror.

What would they do?

Better look the other way readers.

*

"I am aboard ship and lost," Phillipo wanting to thief and pillage.

"I smell the 'Blood of a Filipino," Ronaldo sneaking up behind him.

Does tis mean Filipinos smell bad, past the sell by date, not just these two.

"We must work together to take over this ship Phillipo, think of it as a giant getaway car, no one could stop us," Ronaldo once in control did send his cousin to that arena of Beag built it, if not open a window and shout, "Look it is mummy," and as Phillipo looked, push him out.

And Phillipo knew once he was in control, he did tell his cousin Dorothy was waiting for him below decks. Where it was dimly lit, and no deck existed.

Villains whose middle name was MORIATY.

And while these two plotted a woman with masses of blonde hair tipped the coxswain to 'bugger off.' Because the coxswain was smaller than her, she was able to swing the alien way and being light of build floated towards The Stooges and landed just in front of a cat carrier.

A clawed paw reached out.

And Susanna was now coxswain.

One U.F.O. was just like another.

"Seat belts," she commanded into a microphone and hit a green button.

Sadly, she forgot her own seat belt, so inertia pulled her away into the arms of McSweeny.

"Baby Doll, I knew you cared," and Susanna cringed as

McSweeny to freshen his breath had eaten many of those chili eyeballs as they did not have a price tag on them.

And the mother ship took off, to where, not The United Nations as there was no coxswain.

But there was a film director who had filmed everything and was sitting in a seat with suction pads so made it to the controls.

"Holly Wood," he commanded AUTO PILOT.

And just as well as The Commander in Chief was elderly and dozed off and allowed his fingers to press down on a red button.

Not that one, yes it was that one.

And as the mother ship flew away warheads slammed into the Mohave Desert as no one had told them where to go, or arm them, so nothing was vaporised.

And an old man snoozed on, and his marine made him hot chocolate for when he woke up. She also dropped several sleeping pills in the hot drink. Soon this giant white building in the middle of green lawns did be filled with joyous sounds, squealing girls, party streamers thrown from windows and no one to pick up the dogs what was left on those green manicured lawns.

And the mother ship began to head for the Holly Wood Hills where a film director knew more fame and cash awaited him and explains why he was rubbing his hands in glee.

"Hot chocolate Sir," a waiter approaching him.

And the film director drank the drink and looked at the waiter, he was familiar. "I know you, you are Wayne," and the film director in a panic he had been given arsenic and a lace napkin to wipe his mouth shouted, "Emergency, I need a doctor," and Wayne clicked fingers and little aliens in white doctor overalls came out of the woodwork.

About a hundred, some holding chain saws, others

sledgehammers and others syringes and others jars with chili eyeballs as these aliens liked their snacks.

"I am off," the film director and pressed many buttons he had no idea what they did, so sent a warhead back the home planet, war had just been declared by earth on Planet Ajax.

And a hole in the floor opened and he dropped out, without a parachute.

Is this the end of the man? And Wayne used his dropped camera to film his descent then threw it after him.

"You never liked my cooking," Wayne shouted after him, then held his chin, "wait a moment, he never tried my cooking, what have I done?" So quick thinking threw out a lifeboat disc to attach itself to the unhappy film director who was staring at the ground rushing up to meet him.

Would he make a dent in the soil before the life jacket reached him.

Would he still contact the soil even after the life jacket attached itself to him.

What do you think happened reader?

Beag reached him first.

"How can I ever repay you," the film director thinking of offering Beag the starring role in, 'LEGS,' what else?

And Beag held out a hand with a ringed finger for kissing, he weas an emperor.

The film director hesitated; he was an American.

"What the heck, I kissed worse," and the film director kissed the emperor's ring.

And Beag flew away in his cape crusader outfit, no, in his emperor's outfit with a trailing artificial sable robe.

"That is my Beag," Dorothy watching from the mother ship.

A mother ship now still as it reached the destination of Holly Wood Hills, and Susanna got back to the controls.

Where out came a pocket mirror, hairbrush, foundation,

lipstick, mint mouth spray, arm pit lavender spray, elastic deodorant powder, a clean pair of elastics and bubble gum.

Girls have secret compartments all over their body to hide this stuff and pepper spray, knuckle dusters and nonflexible fingers to poke you in the eyes.

"Where to Dorothy?" Susanna omitting 'empress' as she was an American girl from next door.

"The United Nations," Dorothy.

Below a film director was so busy filming the departure he never heard the silent rubber wheels of a prison van roll right up behind him.

Faces were at the van's window.

I recognise the R.V. owner. As one of those faces.

Is that Diego also.

They could tap on the bus windows and shout to alert the film director of danger.

But the film director never offered them parts in his films as water boys so these two were silent. In fact, their eyes were grim, faces taught, and fists clenched with excitement.

"Hello," a Highway Patrol Officer handcuffing the film director and with help bundled him into the prison van.

Why did Diego and the R.V. owner beat the daylights out of him?

Because prison life is mean.

Yeh, but they had not been tried yet, and 'Working on the Chain Gang' was played over the bus radio and "The Green Mile, showing tonight."

*

So, they PLUMMED themselves banging at the bus windows.

Look at the funny faces they are making, drooling over the dirty windows as their tongues scooped up grim and fingers tried hard to dig a way through reinforced riot proof bus windows.

Hey must be so happy, or they did not be making funny faces so we can leave them.

Who did help them?

And from a porthole in the mother ship Phillipo watched them emotionless. A real Moriarty this one.

Not to worry Ronaldo was aboard ship and had plans foe him so was worse than Moriarty, he was a failed person.

Where was Super Beag, he seems to have a habit of rescuing folks, but Dorothy had not said, "Beag where are you, go help them," for Dorothy remembered Diego's lecherous greasy hands

covered in breadcrumbs and burger mince so he could say things behind the bus window, so she could not hear him.

Do you think he was saying, "Help me," that changed to "Rotten woman, go be a dishwasher," as he realised, she was not helping him and tried to pull back his tongue, but it was stuck on old bubble gum on the window.

Bubble gum some previous passenger had left. Look it has green bits on it.

And the R.V. owner knew from his experiences in the R.V. latrine with pets Dorothy would not recue him so if we lip read, we can make out, "I loath you woman and especially that cat."

And the film director was up front

Repeating these words to the prison bus driver, "I am a film director and can make you a film star, think of the red carpet going into the Oscar Award building for you to walk on, with glorious woman on each elbow, all yours if you stop the bus and let me out, all yours, film star, riches, adored, let me out, stop the bus," very boring repetitive words so the driver fell asleep and the bus driver slept on the door open button.

And the bus collided slowly with a cacti and FREEDOM presented itself to the passengers.

They did not need telling twice and they were gone.

And an empress watched.

She could have shouted, "Off with their heads," but that did mean the mother ship stopping and little green aliens running after the escapees with heavy axes so did never catch them.

*

"Reporting for duty Empress," and said by three folks simultaneously and one was upfront with gold braids on his navy-blue jacket shoulders, masses of them as Mo always over did it.

Behind him Curly Jo and Larry.

Curly Jo held a lead to Jack whose collar was embedded in gems from another world so were valueless on earth.

Larry held a lead to a cat vest made of alien indestructible velvet.

"Walkies," Mo and The Stooges and pets about turned and took a disc down to earth.

You could hear the flapping of Mo's cheeks in the wind.

Then they were down.

Humans with mobiles ran towards them.

"Mummy look what came out of the Corn Flake box," a kid and we will not say any more.

And Philipo aboard ship thought, "One of those discs is better than nothing, I will steal one and be gone on a profitable life of crime."

But BEHOLD, Cousin Ronaldo was eves dropping and what was good for Phillipo was better for him.

So, Phillipo stood beside the glass case in a corridor thinking how to open it and steal the disc in there.

If he had been able to read English he did have read, Emergency lifeboat disc, press green button to activate.

And just like that Fig, a disposed emperor pushed the button and jumped in shutting the glass case behind him, and he gave Phillipo the middle finger.

And just like that Phillipo went berserk and banged on the glass.

And just like that Ronaldo pressed the green button, jumped into the case, and gave Phillipo a middle finger.

Inside the case Fig beat Ronaldo's knees as Fig was a small chap.

Ronaldo laughed as he was a big tough guy.

Then The General pushed the green button and jumped in, so it got cramped in the case.

"I know what to do, press the green button," and Phillipo did and squeezed into the case so there was no room to move.

Fig used his hidden tongue to wrap about a lever and pull it down.

They were off escaping from Empress Dorothy and the tyrant Beag.

Then a green mist filled the case as it zoomed away.

Someone had gassed.

The occupants made funny faces at the windows as they gasped for breath.

And the Empress Dorothy smiled, no one escaped her attention, "Well done General McSweeny," who Saluted her and, in a hand, an empty joke factory bad air canister.

Bad reader for thinking it an empty canister of cyanide, this is a fun tale.

Who said Beag was a tyrant, he was just an adolescent Horney alien, whereas Dorothy was a mature woman. Was she not the one who liked beating the day lights of Diego? No wonder he fled. And the Emperor Fig knew what happened to disposed emperors, they became Wayne's dish washers, what did you think reader, Wayne minced them up as pet food, they were aliens so were pet food RIGHT?

And the overweight General who had been cruel to Beag and Wayne did not want demoted to Private 6th Class Mine Clearance duties, so knew out there troops were still loyal to him, The General.

War was coming to Planet Earth which was not unusual.

And below three folks stopped dead in their tracks, The stooges were in front of them signing autographs so denied responsibility for Freckles and Jack visiting their old friends.

"The leads slipped our hands," these Three Stooges agreed.

It was the screams of terror that brought the human onlookers and bets were laid as to whom Freckles did visit next.

Did we mention Freckles was attired in a feline masked crusader outfit with black paws and fish print on a yellow ochre yellow several piece zip up and a green cape with a print of a smiling cat on it.

And Jack had a spiked collar to add ferocious character as he was a small Jack Russel. Somehow, he was stuffed in a red one piece with holes for whoopsie.

And one of The Stooges carried black pet whoopsie dropping bags.

Which Stooge could it be?

Did you reader say Mo?

Curly Joe?

Leaves one, him complaining heading for slaps.

"I am a film director, get this cat off me," but no one did as no one wanted that cat on them.

"Wish I had a cat like that for a pet," an onlooker said.

"I am a dog person," another.

"Maybe if they dip a paw in this nearby spilt paint, I could get a paw autograph," we will say nothing about this individual.

"Should we phone emergency?" A timid folk.

"What for, I see nothing," a reply.

"I hear nothing," a reply.

"I speak nothing," a reply.

And an empress narrowed her eyes in satisfaction.

An empress about to address The United nations, it went something like this,

"Hello, I am YOUR Empress Dorothy," and the ambassadors seated there thought a mistranslation of what she just said had occurred. *"An Empress," she just said.*

"This is my new home," and showed them on a screen a building being cleared of party goers by aliens dressed as Roman Legionaries. The building looked familiar, *was it you know the one called THE WHITE?"*

Then showed them on the screen the mother ship and a million flying saucers no one in power believed existed, well they did now. *Pity the ambassadors were not allowed to zoom in or did notice 'The Longest Day,' on the film.*

"Where are our forces, be gone Satanic beasts," an ambassador and Dorothy showed them clips from 'The Day of The Triffids,' to make the humans believe earth was in flames. Remember she was a good girl from next door who had made it good in life, she was now the ruler of earth, awesome and all because the lady liked dark chocolate.

Not really but that craving might start, she was ruler because a cute little alien liked her LEGS.

"Hey Beag, I got legs also, come and look," which reader called out that?

And as Dorothy twitched a nose or moved a royal finger and heads were chopped off, no, just kidding, but it was her way of indicating displeasure to Wayne in his attempts to serve up thirty course meals, Dorothy watched her calories but does explain why the human ambassadors who were at her court in that big white house got, can I say it, gross.

And something or someone was missing, something that clings to her LEG.

What was Beag doing these days, well he was flying about earth in his sable robe, mask, and tight fitting one piece and mirror beside him ready to replace those ripping too tight things Beag liked to wear to the "Owe," of earth girls.

He had two hairs growing on his hairless green chest now. He was a man, he had admirers, they all had LEGS.

So Beag rescued many human folks, stopped runaway trams, and took LEGS for a joy ride on his disc where he was heard saying, "LEG."

JUST WAIT TILL THE EMPRESS MET HIM AGAIN?

What do you think Empress Dorothy did do, remember they were not married or playing Monopoly?

What would an earth partner do if she or he found out three were in the relationship, and in this case, billions of earth girls.

But Dorothy knew there was and could only be one LEG, or two LEGS, hers as it was the source of her power. Beag could not go flirting, he was about to meet a woman scorned, "May The Lord Help Him, Amen."

*

And Dorothy saw Beag with a forked tongue plugging a leaky dam on her television.

"We love you Beag," the humans called but she did not hear, "We love Dorothy," well they should have as she never taxed anyone as she was the girl from next door.

And behind her she heard, "Baby Doll, I love you so much, marry me," McSweeny on a knee so his one-piece army green uniform began to rip. Did Dorothy look away, no, sometimes our little girls from next door grow up.

"Is that a **small** diamond in that engagement ring?" Susanna's reply so McSweeny had to peer close. When he looked up Susanna was gone. The point here is, Dorothy was lonely.

"General come here," and McSweeny sat at her feet and the two showed melancholy to the world.

'Nothing Compares to You,' was played over an intercom.

Not even the passing acts of flame and sword swallowers cheered them or the gasping for breath as a sword passed out an exit and flames shot from there.

Courtiers clapped.

Courtiers, yes jealous readers, those that cling to every word you utter and grovel in your footprints on the deep purple carpet.

Not even the trapeze artist missing his target and zooming through a
Window cheered them, nor the lions beating the daylights out of the lion trainer cheered them.

"Let us build an arena and have our citizens fight gladiators to the death," Dorothy and still did not cheer.

"And boil them in giant cauldrons of olive oil," General McSweeny not cheering.

And the courtiers heard and trembled.

"Hello, I am back, miss me?" Beag.

"We are saved, the masked crusader is here," the mistaken courtiers for Beag was already walking amongst them checking LEGS.

And Dorothy fumed.

"Oh, Beag sweetie pie please come here and tell everything about your heroic tales," his Empress Dorothy twitching a finger and folks looked for an executioner, they could understand finger language.

CHAPTER 16 FIG

Nephilim 256 was full of charm like Price. Charming.

Now several unhappy folk had teamed together a SHAKY alliance.

They were that laxative Fig, a right aspirer if ever The Creator Spirit glued together.

That slim figure of a man The General who without

Wayne's rich gravies had lost weight. "Army Field rations," The General hating the dried stuff you added water too to make delicious gruels.

Phillipo, and Ronaldo now green as breathed in the green gas in that escape case and were taken away to a hidden place were aliens who visited ended up, in vials next to interesting piano pieces. What you expect 'body pieces,' remember this is a children's tale. So how did they manage to join the SHAKY alliance of villains?

The green gas eventually left their bodies and the scientists about to dissect them realised , "Hey these two are humans, what idiot sent them to us an aliens? Cur, they stink."

So were given 'hush cash' to keep quiet about what had happened to them, but "They know about us, we will take care of them," MEN IN BLACK.

So, Phillipo and Ronaldo were dumped off at a street corner where the other malcontents had gathered.

"I will be Boss," Phillipo clicking fingers and from alley ways appeared all those on the out skirts of society.

"I will be Boss," Ronaldo clicking his fingers and from cardboard boxes and makes shift tents unkept, unloved folk gathered about him.

These two every now and again threw lower value coins amongst their recruits who tore each other as if Freckles were amongst them and put in extra groans and moans as they knew our most hated villains had green paper money.

And Diego stood aside them, he was aloft to their ways, superior in spirit, having a higher I.Q. and was all rubbish, no MEN IN BLACK had given him bags of cash, and he never asked the fool.

And many 'Light Buzz Years' on toy shop shelves answered the call of their General with the call, "To Infinity and beyond."

Aspirers from across the Galaxies and parallel universes

came riding chariots pulled by goats, cats, horses, bison, and creatures if our Sunday Best folk saw them did call them, "Demons from Hell."

Straight out of Egyptian, Greek, Chinees, Mayan, and the Bags full of museum relics breathing fire and brimstone.

Guess who led them, no guess, give me presents and I will tell you, only fooling, it was handsome boy, me, no, Nephilim

256 and he brought friends, more of his kind so scores of earth girls hung from their tunics, and some so many hanger Ons there managed to pull down the tunics.

"Owe," the on lookers with mobiles.

And these Nephilim did what you and I did do, blush, titter and vamoose. I will tell you for free, sickening it was, hairy moons and knobbly knees and nothing to see as all, almost all wore 'Y' Fronts.

Well, done earth girls who decimated the ranks of these Fallen Angels. It also goes to show we can rely on 'Powder Puff Power,' as the girls hereabouts formed ranks, somersaulting, doing cartwheels, and splits sang 'Heros and Villains,'

And Nephilim 256 tore chunks of his blonde hair from his head and looked well, pure ugly, so his admirers just like that were gone.

"Which leaves me as Emperor Fig," an alien not wanting to reach old age and rock a rocking chair watching the gas rings on Planet Saturn.

And as the plotters argued, a golf ball hit Nephilim 256 on the head.

Then a golf ball hit each head of the afore mentioned twerps above.

A golf buggy stopped near them.

"Fore," a golfer and Emperor Fig swayed then dropped.

Men in Black swarmed over the plotters to depose Emperor Beag and Empress Dorothy in her red shoes, they also swarmed over Fig who was no longer visible. Was that shovels and pick axes at work and when these Men in Black were finished Fig was missing.

A lone yellow plastic daisy was there though on the grass.

"I am me, bow down and worship me, give me your cash donations, your cheer leaders and second mortgages," the golfer and played again and the ball that went high into the clouds and came down on a cute little alien sitting in the grass of a large white house with an open suitcase where his mask crusader too tight outfits spewed forth, also his tooth brush and tooth whitener thrown there by an empress who was wanting to say, "Off with his head," but the Alice in her stopped her. She was still the good American girl that wears a Brownie uniform selling cookies at your door for a hundred a cookie. No wonder she drives an electric scooter with mod cons. A small Brownie uniform on a big girl, smart girl, yes, America is the land of opportunities.

Suddenly a teddy bear span out of a bedroom window and plunked Beag square on.

And from a window curtain slit McSweeny watched and said, "Thank Goodness I am not married," and his baby Doll hearing pushed him from behind, so he fell out the window but was not hurt, remember this is a children's tale as he grabbed the curtain and landed heavily on Beag so never broke any bones.

Never mind about Beag, he provided a soft landing and is an alien, so we do not worry about them slimy tentacle critters that fly about our skies in flying saucers terrifying us.

"We still love you Beag," from adoring crowds outside this large white house as remember Beag stopped runaway trams, lifted sinking fishing boats, and docked them where rescue services handed him medals of bravery.

Beag was a hero to the starved hero-worshipping folk of earth.

And the crowds dispersed as chariots pulled by goats and cats crossed the blue sky.

Grey aliens in flying saucers thrust through white clouds.

Aspirers in an assortment of flying craft in no formation competed with those above to lead the aerial circus show so many collided leaving coloured smoke trails as they fell to earth.

And in a golf buggy a golfer and on the sides of the cart Diego, Phillipo, and Ronaldo at last citizens of a great country's Pine Valley Golf Club.

Where they, did any of us hear them promised that in return for the bags of cash given them by the dissecting scientists, no, I never heard that.

But they were happy in their delusion as were proud citizens with their criminal records wiped clean. *I wonder if they believe the cow jumps over the oon?*

While they could they did write home to their mothers they had made it 'Big Time' in America.

Why just look there was Diego prone making a painful face as he held with fingers a golf ball.

"Fore," the golfer and Diego rolled away holding well what do you think, yes, a red and white stripe candy bar.

And what of the earth generals of earth's armies?

"Remember me," a forgotten Commander in Chief being carried by a party loving female marine. "I lead earth's armies now so call me KING."

"Awesome," and "Owe," and "How much is a hot dog?" From a watching crowd.

"Hey, we do not have KINGS in America, Viv La France and bring back the guillotine," a confused revolutionary.

"Che Guevara," someone not noticing Men in Black with cameras.

"I am John Paul Jones reincarnated," and pranced about in colonial sea faring clothes so they ripped.

"Not boring anymore, the more," the crowd throwing cents to this folk who scooped them up and went to a vendor, a hot dog vendor as this is America.

AND.

Crowds of folk from nowhere produced guns, from pocket, brassiere, under hats, from the inside soles of shoes, and from the hot dog so was dripping ketchup.

"All I said I was KING," The Commander in Chief ducking

bullets.

"Oh Beag, did I hurt you, I am so sorry, here come hug LEG and feel better," a cunning empress knowing Beag, and his mirror was needed to tackle the collection of funnies on her green lawn outside her large white house.

And Beag sucked a toe and held his breath as was sulking.

He was still in puberty and been humiliated in front of his adorers.

And a woman from another realm rode up to him on her chariot and threw a spare cat upon him.

"Oh," his adorers and Beag still did nothing.

Then two goats, Tanngrisnir and Tanngnjostr pulling another chariot stopped at him and began eating what he wore as goats eat anything from tin cans to FIGS.

"Does he have one?"

"Aliens do not have one."

"No wonder his empress threw him out."

And an eight-legged horse, Sleipnir trampled Beag who swayed a bit and his adorers cried and shook their heads, covered themselves in ash and rent their clothes as vendors nearby sold bags of ash and scissors to rent the clothes.

And the rider of the eight-legged horse picked Beag up and laughed and showed him to all.

"They hide their bits," someone.

"He is so cute, why not we stuff him with cotton balls and mass produce him, we did be rich," another.

"Come on Beag, show your worth," a supporter.

"He looks like that thing from 'The Lord of the Rings,'" surely someone who did not like Beag as Beag under that rubber skin was an insect ready to eat humans.

But Beag was limp proving to his fans why Empress Dorothy had bunged him.

And a Ram headed Mannie from another galaxy entered the large white house, so staff inside jumped out windows.

And Dorothy was wrath.

And Susanna was wrath.

And The Stooges appeared and allowed Freckles and Jack to annoy the man on the eight-legged horse.

And this man flicked a finger and sent bolts of lightning into the pets, so they jumped smoking.

And Beag stirred.

He was an animal lover, and they were his pets.

"Gr," escaped his throat.

"What did Beag say?" On lookers.

"He was clearing his throat," one.

"How disgusting," someone not a Beag fan.

And the rider of the horse held Beag to an ear to hear better and was the last he remembered as Beag levitated him to The Bermuda Triangle.

"Our Bsag is back," and the crowd clapped except for Fig digging himself out of soil and his disorientated friends.

And a golfer was about to hit a ball when a magnum was fired and the ball disintegrated, McSweeny had recovered his broken heart.

And McSweeny walked out in his Star Trek uniform swinging his smoking gun.

"I will take care of this," Nephilim 256," and ran towards McSweeny with his horde of fallen angels.

What do you think McSweeny did?

Run or his life if he was smart?

He had noticed Susanna peeking from a curtain above.

Did not Troy fall because of a woman called Helen with an open Crete cleavage? See Powder Puff Power again, when will men learn, NEVER.

So McSweeny full of True Grit, inspired by lust that is akin to love walked towards the thousands of fallen angels.

And beside him The Three Stooges who knew their hour had come. They were going to an actor's guild in the clouds were not out of work actor went hungry or had to ask another actor.

No more slapping Mo.

And beside them Freckles and Jack.

"Not to worry handsome, Baby Doll is here," and Susanna squeezed McSweeney's cheeks, so they glowed RED.

"Bet that was painful," someone eating popcorn.

"Naw is true love," another eating a chili sausage.

And if McSweeny swelled his chest any the more the more he did burst, oh gawd we do not want that gore in this respectable tale, do we?

Who said we do?

And an empress drew back the curtains and stood there legs apart, so her green muslin dress flowed in a soft summer breeze between her legs.

And Beag saw and said, "LEG, "and was a growl.

"Owe," an on looker satisfied now that soft porn had compensated for no gore.

"Leg," Beag growled facing the bad guys.

And a mirror flew beside him with the flag of the United Nations on her, nope, it was The Stars and Stripes. A clock chimed from mirror and a miniature cuckoo clock band circled her playing 'High Noon.'

"Hey boys and girls, what can one puny punk emperor called Beag do to us?" And was the sleepy Commander in Chief being carried on the shoulders of the female marine and was not listened to by the other bad guys.

Why, a revolution was going on about him as folks tired to shred him as America does not have KINGS.

Just as well as Julius Caesar said, "Divide and Rule and to the victor the spoils, for it meant the bad guys were fighting amongst themselves as to whom should be the next emperor instead of fighting as one against Beag.

And a junior flying saucer took to the air and at the controls a mad woman whose blonde hair flowed back in Jetstream, and her clothes were peeling off as Susanna had the wind screen down and knew her business, there were folks that were ogling her when they should have been fighting.

"That is my Baby Doll," McSweeny leading the charge.

What a charge it was, glorious, standards flying, trumpets blaring, men cursing, and canons booming and all rot.

"Hiss," went Freckles at the end of her led jumping onto Nephilim 256 who of course said, "Not again," so fled as his moons showed from clawed black tight P.V.C. fittings.

"Woof," Jack shaking Emperor Fig, so everything hidden by green alien sin popped out this way and that so on lookers covered their eyes and stopped eating hot dogs dripping ketchup.

And "Slapping," was heard often and The Three Stooges slapped their way after the heroic pets.

And McSweeny blasted his magnums and hot nothing, but the sound was terrifying to the enemy for Dorothy to inspire and make an illusion of strength played, "1812," so twelve pounders boomed often.

And what did Beag do?

Well, he was no longer sucking a thumb or holding his breath as boys at his age when sulking become vandals, so he levitated amongst the enemy levitating them, so they spiralled to land ion the sea with splashes.

And mirror produced images of fire breathing dragons and Frost Giants, so the enemy fled.

"I think I am leaving," Phillipo sneaking away but Beag saw him and levitated him to a nearby prison bus that the story demands is here at this exact spot.

And that explains why that bus filled with Ronaldo, Diego, Fig, The Commander in Chief and Nephilim 256 and an aspirer who was almost forgotten so could have escaped but nope, into the prison bus.

There were a lot of buses as there were a lot of work for Beag, Superhero to fill.

"Hi Ho Hi, Ho off to work we go," a prison bus driver sang heading to a prison mail room where mail bags needed sewed.

CHAPTER 17 END

Wayne's wedding cake

And a film director was in his studio editing his mobile phone film and said to himself, "The Man in the Moon," I will call this film and have a tough actor play the main part.

And unwittingly was a propaganda film for Dorothy and not the other bad guys as though action actors are always the heroes.

Did he have a part for Beag, yes, he borrowed a 'Gollum,' type skinny naked creature from The Lord of the Rings as Beag.

Why, because Beag was an alien, and we cannot have aliens playing the main hero. They are the comical side kick that takes the beating the tough actor should have got, the side kick who rides a smaller tricycle while the tough actor speeds about in a black vehicle shooting flames from the exhausts. A miracle

HYBRID, COMEDY SCIENCE FICTION

vehicle as can fly and be a boat or submarine.

And that is why the side kick is depicted as Beag, a Gollum figure of ridicule, and who ever played this part needed to be super fit.

Something tells us this film director did not like aliens, let us ask him why.

And the film director pulled off a rubber face mask and masses of red hair billowed down a well-built ladies frontage, the film director was a girl, not the one from next door, but a girl.

And the R.V. owner stood outside a R.V. show room and was going to buy the biggest R.V. built full of mod cons.

"Do I get to keep the girl?" He asked as all good vehicles show rooms have a semi naked woman sprawled across the R.V. roof and a distraction to a potential buyer as not to notice the high mileage on the speedo.

And he did not get to keep the girl but did drive away in his R.V.

And a vehicle salesman watched him go and a little gird tugged his
 plaid jacket.

"Not now Matilda, Daddy just made a sale."

There was a loud bang and cloud of dense black smoke in the distance.

*

And what about the United Nations?

The ambassadors had pastel coloured skins, tentacles,

they were aliens, but what about the human ambassadors, replaced by these child eaters, aliens that abduct your wives and look, human female short hand secretaries sitting beside them polishing their nails and taking out hair curlers, proof that they have your wives and what stunning looking women so are they

really your wives who have brought up sixteen of your kids, lost their shape so are mistaken for a sack of potatoes?

And where are the human ambassadors?

In cafes fuming over why they were replaced?

Bet you can answer for them?

And a woman at the controls of a junior flying craft sped by, hey, what woman at the controls?

And in the spacious latrine Susanna powder puffed her cheeks a deep red, sprinkled purple oil paint onto her gair and mixed, stuck false vampire teeth in her gums and sprayed garlic essence into her mouth.

"That's Amore," she sang to mirror.

Mirror, hey, should you not be with Beag?

"I like it here; besides I am invited to a wedding," and Mirror giggled.

And below on earth peace rained as angels above had become fed up with humans and taken things into their own hands, IF ONLY. Peace rained as Beg had driven all he bad guys to cafes where they plotted their return.

So McSweeny in a varnished Star Trek Admiral uniform waited at the alter placed in a meadow flower filled park.

The Three Stooges gleamed hair gel and that stuff some

folk smell clean always while you stink of body odour.

The pets had been groomed.

They were content to behave for they could see pet bowls ahead, bowls full of Southern fried chickens that were about to flee in a 'Great Escape.'

See even chickens have brains.

And The Empress Dorothy was next to McSweeny.

And who was to give Susanna away, Beag of course if he was here.

So where was he, at the entrance to the park posing for mobile phone snaps and signing autographs but the adoring mob stripped him for souvenirs, so Beag fled into a water barrel left out for days, so he shared it with mosquito larvae and that is how he went to the wedding.

As a male alien teenager, he had thousands of images of LEGS in his mind. Hey, wait a moment, we do not even know how aliens well phone the stork for babies. But if those Greys and Nephilim's are any idea we can guess.

Bad Beag, you have an empress waiting for you, yes waiting to beat the daylights out of you.

ANYWAY.

Susanna was not at the controls so explains why her craft took the roofs of those prison buses and those inside looked at the sky and climbed out.

"Stop or I will shoot," the prison guards but seeing the savage prisoners changed their words to, "Just joking, bye and please write."

So, the contents of a continuation are free.

And Susanna smudged the black lipstick with those bumps on the bus roofs across her cheeks.

And left it with these words, "He never waited for a reply, the cave man, so I better turn up for my wedding," and grinned showing multi painted teeth.

"All the better to kiss," she mused.

And landed at the top of the red carpet and jumped out billowing a noticeably short skirt.

"Owe," the on lookers thinking McSweeny was a lucky fella.

The band started playing, 'Here Comes the Bride,' all the squeezed in guests sighed as you do at weddings.

Out came the paper hankies, the confetti began to rain down, bridesmaids somersaulted to Suanna's side to hold up a non-existent dress tail and froze. A sad thing to do when performing acrobatic feats so ended up on guests.

Were there complaints, listen we are dealing with the Sons of Adam here.

Susanna's truly short skirt was too short, her covered moons wee showing.

And Susanna opened her mouth and waved at the guests who began fainting.

McSweeny trembled, what was he marrying, someone worse than himself so he spoke to his GUN.

And gun remained silent as our guns do not have Ai yet.

And Susanna jumped onto him and smooched.

What happened?

McSweeny fled but Susanna still smooched.

"Marry me Empress Dorothy," a voice from a water barrel.

And Empress Dorothy was not amused, would you.

And Susanna came back minus McSweeny, "Is a woman's prerogative to change her mind," she said and at this Dorothy could agree so took her anger out on a water barrel, so the guests were not disappointed for coming to this wedding.

There would be dancing, eating and Wayne was cooking, and it was a happy occasion, people ate and drank too much so do not be surprised babies were made.

That big white house had many guest rooms.

And Dorothy handed Beag a paper napkin to cover his vitals.

Earth had an empress, emperor, and peace.

"God bless the aliens who gave it to us as we never gave it to us, a FOX anchor man.

And in the meadow of flowers McSweeny pulled the petals of bee food with these words, "She loves me, she loves me not," and ended on?

THE END

Printed in Great Britain
by Amazon